An Elemental Water

Book 3 of
The Ardraci Elementals

Carol R. Ward

An Elemental Water
ISBN 978-1-937477-25-7
An Elemental Water Copyright © 2014 Carol R. Ward
Published by Brazen Snake Books

This book is a work of fiction and any resemblance to persons, living or dead, or places, events or locales is purely coincidental. The characters are productions of the author's imagination, and used fictitiously.

Dedication

For Steve, who puts up with me.

Acknowledgments

A special thank you to Jamie DeBree, who's never afraid to tell me the truth. That's a rare quality these days. Her talents know no bounds, as the cover art she created for me proves. Thank you as well to Steve and Catherine for their insightful comments that were indispensable during the editing process.

Chapter One

From Nereida's Journal:

My name is Nereida. I have no last name - none of us do. My life has been a string of secrets and things I'm not supposed to know. Like, my mother's name was Namir. I'm not supposed to know that, but I do. I'm also not supposed to remember that I have a twin brother, or know that we have a younger sister. And I'm not supposed to know that my mother died to give our sister a chance at freedom. The fact that my brother, Kairavini, and I can speak mind to mind is one of the biggest secrets. I don't know what would happen if they ever found out. But as close as we are, even Ravi doesn't know my deepest secret. I am an Ilarie, a vessel. I carry within me the soul, as you would put it, of the Illezie Sta'at. But I'm getting ahead of myself.

The night was absolute. The door to the small room was sealed tight and there were no windows to let in a hint of moonlight. It was dark and quiet, but something was amiss.

Despair.

Hopelessness.

Fear.

Kairavini woke from a sound sleep and sat up with a gasp. *Nereida!*

There was no answer. It was the emotions he was sensing, not actual words. Something was terribly wrong. He could feel it in his gut.

Nereida, what's happened? Please talk to me!

There was no answer, but he could sense his sister's mental anguish. Ravi didn't hesitate. Throwing back the covers he got out of bed and left his room.

The lights in the corridor were dim, but it didn't impede him in the least. He could find his way to Nereida's room blindfolded if he had to, despite her insistence that he stay away.

The corridors were deserted - only the labs and restricted areas were well guarded, the living quarters had only a cursory guard. Ravi looked around quickly before he paused outside the door and knocked gently.

"Nereida," he whispered. "Are you in there?"

He tried the handle -- it was unlocked. Easing it open he took a step inside and tried again. "Nereida?"

There was a whimper from the far side of the room. He moved forward in the dark until he hit the bed, then felt gingerly around until he located the lump huddled in the center.

"Nereida, everything will be all right." He pulled her into his arms. "I'm here now."

"Kairavini?" She sounded confused as she struggled to wake up.

"You were having a nightmare, a really bad one."

"Ravi? What are you doing here?" Her voice was stronger and she pulled away from him. "You can't be here Ravi, you need to go."

"Not until I know you're all right. Lights at thirty per cent."

"No!" Nereida said at the same time the automatic control turned the lights on low. She tried to hide as Ravi gasped.

"Oh, my sister, what has happened to you?"

Almost a year had passed since they'd undergone their *tespiro*, the phase of their life that gave them the ability to become full Elementals. Many died during this time. It was both a terrifying and painful rite of passage. Until this moment he had not realized the toll it had taken on his sister.

He pulled her painfully thin form back into his arms, tears pricking at his eyes as she began to cry. Rocking her back and forth he stroked her hair at the same time, whispering words of comfort. He flashed back to his *tespiro*, to being in the infirmary, to the emaciated figure he thought he'd glimpsed in a second tub of saline solution. Remembered the voices he'd overheard, that the female was not to be given the drugs that would ease her passage.

"It was you, wasn't it? They were going to let you die. But why?"

"My gift is very weak, just like me."

"Why didn't you tell me?"

"There was nothing you could have done; I didn't want to upset you."

"We could leave this place. We could--"

"And do what, go where?" She pulled away from him and swiped her arm across her eyes. "Even if we were to venture outside we have no idea what direction the nearest people are, nor how far they would be. We would die out there."

He sighed. "It was just a thought. Perhaps some day . . ."

It was her turn to sigh. "Just leave it, Ravi. You can't change the past, you can only look towards the future."

"All right, if that's what you want," he agreed reluctantly. "Do you want to talk about what got you so upset tonight?"

She shuddered. "It was a dream, unlike any other I've had before. I couldn't seem to wake up and it terrified me."

He took her thin hand in his. "Tell me."

"It seemed so real at the time, like I was living it. But now I can only remember bits and pieces. There was fire, a terrible fire. And explosions, the ground was shaking. I think the volcano was erupting. There was this girl . . . she seemed familiar somehow. And a man who belonged to her. He was standing in flames . . ."

"Do you know how far into the future this could be?"

"I have no idea," she admitted. "It could be days, it could be years. But the one thing I'm certain of, many people are going to die."

Ravi stayed with Nereida until she fell into what he hoped was a dreamless sleep, then slipped away back to his own room before he was missed. For tonight at least the dim corridors lost their adventurous appeal, instead they had an ominous feel and he found himself jumping nervously at shadows. When he was finally safe in bed he found his own sleep to be elusive.

He couldn't believe that those in authority had been prepared to let Nereida die, just because her gift wasn't strong enough. Even more, he couldn't believe Nereida had kept something like this from him. But then again, maybe he could understand her reasoning. She knew that his first reaction would to be get them both away from this place, but as she said, where would they go? It made him wonder, what else had she been keeping from him?

Surely she was not the first with a weak gift, what happened to the others? He tried to remember the different power ratings of the others in his year group - three, five, four . . . he was the only seven. Where were those whose power was less than a three rating? It's not like he could ask an instructor about it. They were there to instruct, not answer questions.

He'd been so proud of being part of the Program, so proud of his power rating. Now he just felt . . . stupid. Stupid and betrayed. For the first time in his life he found himself questioning the whole point of the breeding program.

From the time they'd been taken away from their mother they'd had it drilled into them how important the breeding program was, how privileged they were to be a part of it. Was this really all there was to their lives? Why was it so important that the breeding lines be kept pure? How powerful did an Elemental have to be before it was considered enough, and what would happen to the rest of them when that was accomplished?

Nereida almost died because her gift wasn't strong enough, but that didn't make sense. They were taught that most of those with very weak gifts underwent mild *tespiros*. Why was hers so bad then?

Most of his recollections of that time were of the intense pain he'd felt, snatches of overheard conversations of the doctors as they helped see him through it. He'd lost his connection with her, the intense pain kept them from communicating mind to mind and that made him frantic to know what was going on with her.

At one point they had to restrain him from going to her - he could feel the pain she was in. He recalled an exchange between two technicians about genetic links, though they never guessed about the mind to mind communication. Was it because of that they kept her alive?

Kairavini sat up in bed suddenly. Was that the reason she'd been in such pain to begin with? Because she was experiencing *his* pain? The very idea horrified him. He needed to find one of the medical technicians who oversaw his *tespiro* to ask him about it.

S*top it!* Nereida demanded. *There is nothing to be gained from reliving the past. What's done is done. We cannot ask questions without revealing our mutation --*

*W*hat do you mean, mutation?

A*s far as I'm able to determine, there's never been another set of twins born into the Program. That alone is enough to make us abnormal. But we are able to communicate mind to mind as well. What do you think they would do to us if this were ever discovered?*

An icy chill went up Ravi's spine. *And there are your dreams, your ability to see into the future. I've never heard of anyone else with your ability.*

She made no reply and Ravi sat up even straighter in bed. *Nereida?*

There was one other, she replied. If she'd been speaking out loud her voice would have been a whisper. As it was, her mental voice was a mere wisp.

What happened?

Nereida gave a mental shrug. *She's gone now, that's all that matters. Now, would you stop thinking so hard and go to sleep? I don't know about you, but I have an early day tomorrow.*

Ravi smiled into the dark. *As you wish, sister.* He slid downwards in his bed again.

Kairavini?

Yes, Nereida?

It was good seeing you again.

Chapter Two

From Nereida's Journal:

Sta'at says I should start at the beginning, so I shall. My brother and I were born in a compound made from parts of the ship that brought a man named Uri Arjun and his followers to this world. When we were two, we were taken from our mother and placed in the nursery with the other children from our year group. We never saw our mother again. This was the way of things. We were separated into boys and girls dormitories but we still had a limited amount of play time together, and all of our meals. When we were five, we started classes so that should we not be useful for Dr. Arjun's breeding program, we might be useful in some other way. But the main purpose of Dr. Arjun's compound was to create Breeders and Seeders for his Program.

After everyone in his year group passed their *tespiro*, classes in the art of breeding were added to their schedules, as well as instruction in the use of their element. Kairavini found it increasingly difficult to keep from asking questions during the weekly lectures on the breeding process. In fact, he was beginning to question a great many things about the Program itself, though he was not foolish enough to ask those questions out loud.

The breeding itself was straight forward enough, it was just everything leading up to it that was confusing. The instructor kept emphasizing they were to keep their emotions at bay, but wouldn't having some feelings towards the other person only make the whole thing easier? It was not so much his duty he questioned, it was the execution of that duty.

"I hate to say it," his friend Zephryn told him, after glancing furtively around the dining hall to make sure no one was close enough to listen. "But I have to agree. It's only human nature to have emotions. To tell us we have to do something so . . . intimate and not express any kind of emotion is crazy."

"I'll bet we're not the only ones who feel this way either," Ravi said.

"I wonder why Dr. Arjun doesn't just use artificial means for the breeding?"

"I've never thought about it before, but now you've got me wondering too. If he really didn't want emotions involved, that would be the perfect solution."

"Well, feel free to ask the instructor during the next class," Zephryn said with a grin.

"Ha! Not after what happened to Adan."

Questions were not encouraged during class. Adan, an Earth Elemental who barely rated a three on the power scale, once asked for clarification on several points. Instead of receiving an answer, he received several days of short rations and restricted privileges instead.

Kairavini sat up straighter in his chair and looked around the dining hall.

"What is it?" Zephryn asked

"Have you noticed that only the post-*tespiro* but pre-breeding Seeders use this dining hall?"

"I -" Zephryn stopped and looked around. "I hadn't really thought about it before. So what?"

"I'm just wondering what happens once we're part of the breeding program."

"What do you mean?"

"With all this talk about suppressing our emotions, I'm wondering if we'll be allowed to be friends still."

"Why, because I'm Wind and you're Water?" Zephryn asked.

"No, because they don't want us forming any kind of attachment at all."

Zephryn took another look at the occupants of the dining hall. "I think we should make a pact," he said.

"What kind of pact?" Ravi asked, curious.

"That no matter what happens, we'll always be friends."

"Agreed!"

As they shook hands in agreement the warning sounded for their next class. They took their trays to the disposal unit and then parted ways.

* * * * *

"This will be your last lesson in the use of your element," the instructor told the line of boys standing on the sand. "The intent of these lessons was to teach you control and most of you have accomplished that."

They'd been meeting in this chamber twice a week for the past three months, and their control of their element was deeply ingrained now. Even Ravi was able to complete the exercises as instructed, though he seemed to have to work harder at it than the others. It made him wonder what the rating numbers burned into their arms were really for - his was the highest number, yet he was having the most trouble, so obviously the higher the number didn't necessarily mean the largest gift.

"Today you will manipulate your element in its natural environment. Think of it as your final exam."

There was a general restless shifting along the line, but no one was quite brave enough to ask what would happen if they failed. Would they be removed from the breeding program? Banished from the facility? Failure was not an option.

Ravi tried to pay attention, but the instructor had one of those sonorous voices that tended to make him sleepy. It was a good thing they were standing, otherwise he'd have nodded off by the time the man was finished.

After the Water Elemental finished his lecture, he had the boys come up one by one to stand beside him at the edge of the water. They were to reach out with their senses and embrace their element, seeking out its source and drawing it towards them in the form of a small wave.

There were several false starts, and a boy who'd been advanced ahead of his year group got their feet wet when the wave he created slapped into the shore when it was released. All too soon it was Ravi's turn and he swallowed hard as he approached the edge of the water.

"There's nothing to worry about," the instructor told him with an unexpected show of sympathy. "Just reach out with your mind and feel the water. Follow it to its source and then draw it gently towards you."

Ravi nodded. He squared his shoulders and faced the water. Shutting his eyes he cleared his mind of everything but the task ahead. He could sense the water in front of him; what they saw in the chamber was only a small part of it.

"Just relax and give it a try," the instructor encouraged him.

Ignoring him, Ravi reached for the vast expanse of water and started to draw it towards him. He pulled, and pulled, and pulled, wanting to impress the instructor with this last assignment. Dimly he heard yelling, but he was too focused on his task to pay attention.

Something slammed into him hard, breaking his concentration, and he fell, losing control of the water he'd been manipulating. His eyes snapped open and caught just a glimpse of a gigantic wave before it broke, drenching everyone in the chamber.

The instructor held out a sodden hand to help him up. "Are you all right?" Ravi nodded, still not sure what had happened. "I didn't mean to shove you so hard, but you were about to drown us all."

Ravi's eyes widened. He looked from the instructor to the line of dripping boys to the pool of water, still in movement from the aftershocks of the wave collapsing.

"That concludes your lessons on controlling your element. You will all follow me back to the facility and from there disperse to your rooms for meditation."

The line of boys began filing by, several of them glancing curiously at Ravi as he stood rooted in place, trying to figure out whether what he'd done was considered impressive or disastrous. A couple of them glared at him for the wetting they'd taken, and the youngest grinned at him, mouthing the word, "spectacular."

With a resigned sigh, Ravi fell in step behind them, lagging behind slightly. When they reached the place where the tunnels branched, he paused, pretending to check his shoe for a stone. As the voices faded away, he ducked into the side passage, one hand on the wall to feel his way.

One of Ravi's greatest failings, as he was told many times by his sister, was his insatiable curiosity. It was his curiosity that led him to choose security systems as an independent study, studies students were allowed to undertake without supervision. Surprisingly, his subject matter was not flagged by the system, probably because he focused on physical locks rather than electronic security. He became quite adept at getting around locks of every description, which allowed him to explore the compound after lockdown at night.

For three months now he'd been burning with curiosity as to what lay down this passage; why the other one had been chosen for the lessons instead of this one. The one lock he had yet to master was the electronic lock on the metal door separating the personal quarters from the rest of the mountain. This might be his only chance to satisfy his curiosity. And that curiosity was stronger than ever after the amount of water he'd sensed when being tested.

After shuffling several feet down this new tunnel he decided it was safe enough, and reached into his pocket for the hand held artificial light he'd pilfered from a store room the night before. The light it emitted wasn't overly bright, but it was enough to show that this passage was much like all the others, albeit somewhat narrower. He followed as it snaked its way almost parallel to the one they used to get to the training room. There was a bend in this tunnel, however, and just past the bend the rock under foot turned to sand as the tunnel opened up into a large chamber.

Ravi's breath caught in his throat and he stared in awe. The chamber was enormous, filled with a soft glow from the multi-colored, phosphorescent moss covering the stalactites. His light reflected back at him from clear crystals embedded in the walls and ceiling of the chamber and he pointed it downwards, at the fine black sand under his feet.

The chamber must be millions of years old, he thought. Several enormous stalagmites were poking up through the pool of water spread out before him, and he had to wonder just how deep the water went. It never occurred to him to use his gift to find out.

He knew it wouldn't be long before he was missed, but he vowed he'd come back to this chamber again, and often. Just as soon as he figured out how to bypass the security door. Maybe he could even persuade Nereida to come with him - she'd love to see this.

Retracing his steps to the join in the tunnels, he stooped down and removed one of his shoes, pitching it into the darkness of the passage that lead to the elemental classroom. Switching off his light, he stowed it in his pocket and stumbled his way to the dimly lit, main passage. He could hear voices coming from it and schooled his face into what he hoped was a worried, yet contrite expression. The instructor, as well as three security guards, met him in the passage.

"I lost my shoe," he said, a quaver in his voice. "And then everyone was gone and I tried to hurry but I tripped and then I got turned around and I was afraid I'd get lost forever."

The security guards glared at him, one brushing by to check further down the passage. The leader opened his mouth to speak but the Elemental pushed him aside. "I did warn you boys to stay close," he said mildly. "Are you all right?"

"Yes sir," Ravi said, gaze lowered, toe of the foot that still had its shoe scuffing in the dirt covering the rock of the passage. "I'm just glad you found me."

The security guard returned, holding Ravi's shoe in his hand, and nodded briefly to the one in charge. "Broken fastening," he said. The leader examined the shoe and then handed it to Ravi.

"There, no harm done," the Elemental said. "As I've said before, these caves are no place to be wandering around in. Perhaps you would be wise to check your other footwear for damage when you return to your quarters for meditation."

"Yes, sir," Ravi agreed fervently. There was something else going on here, something that had nothing to do with him and his shoe. He could tell by the looks the guards exchanged and the false cheerfulness of the Elemental's voice. For now he'd just file it away for future reference.

Chapter Three

From Nereida's Journal:

When we were ten, Dr. Arjun found it necessary to move the compound to a more secure location. Despite ships of any kind being prohibited on this world, we were herded, in the dead of night, onto transport ships that took us to our new home. You have no idea what a traumatic experience this was for children who had never been outside before. While the old compound had been close to a town, the new one was set against the side of a dormant volcano so that Dr. Arjun could take advantage of the natural cave system within. He also took this opportunity to inform us that we would no longer be known by names, only designations, which were burned into the skin of our wrists. These showed at a glance what our generation number and result numbers were, and whether we were an Elemental or a Mistake. Kairavini was a potential Elemental. His designation was AE-03-85, meaning he was the 85th child born of third generation aquatics. A power rating of 07 was added *after he passed through his tespiro. My designation is AEM-177, meaning I was also a potential aquatic but of insignificant use to the Program. In other words, I was a mistake.*

"You're late," Dr. Arjun stated.

The Water Elemental standing in front shifted uncomfortably. "It couldn't be helped, sir. One of the boys became lost in the caves on the way back to the compound."

"And you're late with your report."

"Yes sir, as I said I--"

"Which boy?"

"Which boy sir?" Sweat broke out on his forehead.

"Which boy became lost in the caves?"

"Oh. Sorry, sir. It was AE-03-85-07, sir."

"Ah, yes." The doctor flipped through the report on his desk. "And how did he fare in his classes?"

"He was quite amazing," the Elemental told him eagerly. "He excelled at all his tasks, surpassing the others by a wide margin. His final test . . . he could have drowned us all. I've never seen anything like it. I can only imagine what he could do with a larger body of water and without the inhibitor."

"Indeed."

The doctor's tone of voice curbed the Elemental's enthusiasm as nothing else could.

"I--that is--not that it matters, really. I--"

"Kindly cease your babbling. You have done well. You are dismissed."

"Yes sir, thank you sir."

The Elemental's relief was palpable. Arjun wouldn't have been surprised to see the man bow his way out the door. After the man was gone there was a sharp rap on the door.

"Come."

The head of security entered and stood in almost the same spot the Elemental had been in. He was calm and ice cold where the Elemental had been nervous sweat.

"Report."

"There was a disturbance in the caves. One of the boys became lost on the way back from their lessons."

"So I've heard. The most powerful Elemental to come out of the program to date, and he got lost. Would you say it was deliberate or accidental?"

The security guard hesitated. "It appears to have been accidental."

"Appears to have been?"

"The boy was the last in line; his shoe had a worn fastening. When he stopped to adjust it the others went ahead without realizing he'd fallen behind. As the Elemental pointed out, it's easy to get turned around in the dark."

"Hmm. Do you think the Elemental might be covering for the boy?"

# #

Again the guard hesitated. "It's doubtful sir, but he was acting suspicious. He seemed to be trying to hurry us out of there."

"Do you think he knows?"

"If he doesn't, then he at least suspects."

"Very well. You'll take care of the matter, won't you?"

"Of course sir."

"Good." Dr. Arjun opened a drawer of his desk and took a folder out. "Now, it appears as though I'll need a new Water Elemental to instruct the next group of boys."

* * * * *

There was no graduation ceremony for Ravi's year-group when they reached the completion of their classes. Instead they were informed when the last day of formal classes would be, and given a list of expectations of how they were to conduct themselves from that time forward.

"Look at this," Ravi said to Zephryn as they sat at a table together in the dining hall for what was probably the last time. He held out his tablet for Zephryn to see, even though there was an identical one in front of him. "We will no longer be taking our meals in the dining hall. They'll be delivered to us in our rooms."

"You were right," Zephryn told him. "They don't want us socializing."

"It just doesn't make sense," Ravi said. "And it's not fair."

Zephryn looked around to make sure no one was within listening distance. "The Wind Elemental who taught us, he told us . . ."

"Told you what?"

"He said we should try not to let ourselves become too isolated. It isn't the way we were supposed to live."

"We don't really have much choice, that's just the way it is."

"And he said . . . when it comes to the breeding it's easier if you do engage your emotions, just make sure you don't become attached to the breeder."

"Huh." Ravi sat back in his chair. "It's what we suspected all along. I just don't understand why they think no emotions is better."

"I don't know," Zephryn said. "But he told us breeding was more than just a biological function and it was wrong to teach us otherwise."

"He told you that?"

"Well," Zephryn looked a little shamefaced. "I may have overheard him talking to someone else. But I found this," he held out an information crystal. "It fell out of his pocket."

"What's on it?"

Again Zephryn looked furtively around the room. "Information, stories, illustrations. It's about other worlds and how people live on them. It--it's so much . . . more than we've been led to believe."

Ravi took the crystal from him and turned it around in his hands. "Where do you suppose he got it?"

"I don't know. But the stories on there make me feel . . . I don't know."

Passing the cube back, Ravi said, "You need to get rid of this before you get caught."

"I know. I'm going to. I'm afraid to keep it any longer. The Wind Elemental is gone, just like that instructor that gave us the access codes for our independent studies."

Frowning, Ravi tried to remember the last time he'd seen the Water Elemental that taught his group. "Maybe they were only here to teach us, and when they were finished they went back to wherever they came from."

"Do you really believe that?"

They stared at each other across the table. "No," Ravi said finally, shaking his head. "But I do believe we'd better change the topic."

Zephryn took a sip of the hot drink in front of him. "So . . . no more formal instruction. We're adults now."

"Funny, I don't feel different."

"Me either. I wonder if that'll change after we've become experienced at breeding?"

"I don't know, I just wish I could just get it over with," Ravi told him.

"I wonder if it'll be anyone I know?" Zephryn mused.

"What do you mean?"

"You know, from our year group. We used to have our meals with a few of the breeders. What if we're paired with one of them? Like, what if you're paired with that Nereida you were always hanging around with? I don't remember her designation but I think she was water."

Ravi had just taken a large gulp of his drink and ended up spewing it all over the table. "That's--that's--" He forced himself to calm down and reminded himself that there was no way Zephryn could know Nereida was his sister.

"I guess that answers that question," Zephryn said with a grin. "For what it's worth, I think it would be easier with a stranger than someone I know too."

"How's your independent study on flight going?" Ravi asked, deliberately changing the subject. Apparently airships were another safe subject to study independently. It's not like they'd ever have access to one. And even if they did, where would they fly to?

Ravi allowed mind to wander as his friend launched into a description of the mechanics of the machines that allowed men to fly. He couldn't help wondering though, what would that first breeding be like?

Chapter Four

From Nereida's Journal:

Sta'at says I must talk about my tespiro, which happened at the same time as Ravi's. Unlike puberty where the body changes happen at different ages and are different for males and females, tespiro is much the same for everyone and occurs around the age of sixteen. This is the transition where we come into our elemental power. Sta'at says that on Ardraci, where our people originated, tespiro only lasts a few days at best. But here, because of all the genetic manipulation we've undergone, a tespiro can last for more than a week. Kairavini's tespiro lasted fifteen days - the longest on record. But while he was given drugs and baths in saline solutions to help ease his transition, I was not. Though I shared his pain I did not share his power. If it had not been for the strong mental link between us, they would have just let me die. But they were afraid that if I died so would he, and they could not afford to lose such a powerful Elemental.

Kairavini paced in his room. He'd received his notification this morning that he was scheduled for a breeding this afternoon. There had to be something unnatural about him. This was something he was supposed to be looking forward to, but instead he was dreading it. It was what he'd been bred for, it was time he fulfilled his purpose.

He wished he had someone to talk to about it, at this point he'd even talk to Zephryn. He hadn't seen his friend in six months, not since they'd reached the age of breeding. Just like he'd predicted, they were no longer allowed to associate with each other. Well, that wasn't precisely the truth. It wasn't so much they weren't allowed, there was just no longer any opportunity.

With each successive milestone they became more and more isolated. At two they were taken from their mothers and placed in a nursery, and then at five separated into boys and girls dormitories. Kairavini and Nereida had classes together until they hit puberty, when once again they'd been segregated into boys and girls classes, although they were still able to meet in the dining hall.

After *tespiro*, however, socialization between males and females was strictly forbidden, and all other social interaction was done under the watchful eyes of the attendants in the dining halls. Now that they were Seeders, even that was taken away from them. While it was not forbidden to be found outside their rooms, neither was it encouraged.

D*o you know what today is?*

Shocked at the sound of his sister's voice in his head, Ravi stopped pacing. Of all the times she could have contacted him, this was the worst possible.

I*t's the anniversary of our birth*, she continued. *We were born nineteen years ago. I have been researching birth customs of other cultures and some celebrate this day every year. They call it a birth day.*

A *birth day? What a strange thing to celebrate. Birth is a natural biological function.* Ravi was just grateful that she didn't pick up on what was really on his mind.

P*art of the celebration is the giving of gifts and the eating of cake. And you'll never guess what they put on the cake.*

W*hat do they put on the cake?* Ravi asked, humoring her.

W*ax candles. They light the candles and the one who's birth day it is blows out the flames. Isn't that the oddest thing you've ever heard of?*

I *wonder why they do it.*

I *don't know. Perhaps their eyesight is very dim and they need the extra light to see.*

B*ut then why blow them out again?*

A sigh filled his mind. *I don't know.*

She paused for so long he thought she'd wandered off, so when she spoke again he gave a start of surprise. *You don't need to work so hard shielding your mind from me. I know what you'll be doing in a little while.*

Y*ou do?* He wanted to sink right through the stone floor.

T*here's nothing to be embarrassed about, it's what we were bred to do. It's perfectly natural.*

Ravi resumed his pacing. *That's just the problem. I don't feel like it's natural at all. It's unnatural for two people who've never met to do something so intimate together. At least it looks pretty intimate - you do it without any clothing, and there's naked flesh touching naked flesh, and--*

R*avi!*

He winced as Nereida's mind-voice cut him off in mid-babble.

Y*ou have to move past this, Ravi. I've never heard of anyone refusing to do their duty but I'm sure the punishment would be terrible.*

I*'m not intending to refuse,* he replied. *I just wish I could get it over with.*

I*f you don't relax, you may not be able to do your duty.*

O*h, thank you, that makes me feel so much better.*

I*'m serious Ravi, you have to relax. It's not as bad as you're making it out to be.*

A*nd how would you know?*

The voice in his mind went silent. Ravi stopped pacing again.

W*e're nineteen years old, you said. The breeding age for females was lowered to eighteen. You've already done this, haven't you?*

Still, Nereida was silent.

If it's not so bad, then why didn't you tell me?

* * * * *

Nereida sat on her bed in her room, arms wrapped around her knees.

It's different for females than it is for males, she told her brother finally. That much was certainly true. *What would you have had me say? It's not something you slip into casual conversation.*

In her mind she could picture Ravi sitting down on the bed in his own room, unconsciously mimicking her pose. *I guess I don't know what you could have said. I just . . . I just don't like the thought of . . .* She felt the coldness in his gut as he tried to think of breeding from her point of view. *Okay, I guess I understand why you didn't say anything.*

Thank you.

Can I ask you how long . . . never mind, it's none of my business.

Shortly after the eighteenth anniversary of our birth, she said, figuring out what he wanted to know.

At least I know everything went all right for you.

How would you know that? she asked, startled.

I don't recall sensing any extreme emotions coming from you.

Oh. Like I said, it's different for females. Different enough that she had learned how to block her brother almost entirely from her thoughts and certainly from her emotions.

It was especially different for the M class like her. She hoped her brother never found out just how different it was. It was only good fortune that her first time had taken place while Ravi was off in the shielded cave training his element.

The M class was not part of the breeding program. In the old compound they would have been quietly disposed of, but in this dark, isolated place Dr. Arjun found a new use for them. Even land craft were not allowed on this world and with the nearest town over a day's journey by horse, it left very little in the way of entertainment for the security guards. The women, and men, with the M class designation were the perfect solution.

Once she was fully recovered from her *tespiro*, Nereida was told what her role would be in the organization. Since she did not qualify to become a medical or laboratory technician she would be made available to individuals of the security team for their pleasure. Her other choice was to leave the compound, which was impossible. Even if she knew of a way to survive on the outside, she could not leave her brother behind.

The classes in sexuality for those with the M designation, male and female together, were much different than the classes given those in the breeding program. The emphasis here was on the giving of pleasure, not procreation. There was no concern of un-wanted pregnancy; since their DNA was of no use to the breeding program, they were sterilized.

What if I'm not able to do what I'm supposed to do? Ravi asked her suddenly.

She started and brought her mind back to the present. *Do not fret, brother. They will make sure you're able to do what you need to do.*

How? he asked, surprised.

It's reassuring that no matter what else happens to us, some things never change. You failed to pay attention in class, Ravi. Despite the fact the M class were not used for breeding, they were well aware what happened to those in the program. *The first few times you will be given a drug that will ensure you're able to do your duty. And you'll be paired with an experienced breeder who will help guide you.*

In his room, Ravi shivered. *It sounds so . . . so . . .*

Nereida sighed. *It is what it is, brother. There's not much anyone can do about it except endure.*

Is that what you do? Endure?

Kairavini . . . her mind's voice was laced with warning.

Sorry, he said meekly, and quickly changed the subject. *They say we are to keep our emotions at bay. I do not know how this is possible.*

It's not, she said bluntly. *But you need only make sure you do not form an attachment.*

She knew from the spike in his emotions that the guard had arrived to take him to his breeding. *You will be fine, brother.*

He did not seem at all reassured as the guard led him away.

T*he breeder they pair you with will be lucky to have you*, she added, almost too softly for his mind to hear.

Chapter Five

From Nereida's Journal:

Most of the things I write of here are in the past and I am of a mind to leave them there. But it is important that I share certain things so that you many see how my life was shaped. It will also help you understand why Sta'at has become so important to me. After tespiro, when it was confirmed I would not be part of the breeding program, I was put into special classes with the rest of the M-class. We had little or no aptitude for science, so we could not become lab technicians, and the security guards are mercenaries hired from without. The only thing we were considered fit for was stress relief for the guards. Sta'at says that is a polite way of saying we were forced into sexual slavery. So while my brother learned about the act of procreation and had it drilled into him that the process should be undertaken without emotion, I was taught how to please a man through various sex acts. Ironically, emotion did not enter into our task either. But that is because no one cared how we felt being used so.

Ravi swallowed hard as the guard knocked on the door and then opened it for him. He stepped inside and took a moment for his eyes to adjust to the dimmer light. The woman - after talking with Nereida he couldn't think of her as just a Breeder - was sitting on the bed, but got up and approached when it appeared his feet were frozen to the floor.

She was about the same height as he was, with the same blue eyes and blonde hair, but more slender. Nereida had said the Breeder would be experienced, which probably meant older, but he had no frame of reference to judge her age.

"What's your name?" she asked.

"AE-"

"No," she said shaking her head. "I didn't ask for your designation, I asked for your name."

"I thought we weren't . . . Kairavini. My name is Kairavini."

She smiled at him. "I'd tell you there's no need to be nervous, Kairavini, but the first time is always nerve-wracking."

Taking him by the hand she pulled him over to the bed and then pushed him down into a sitting position.

"Here, drink this." She handed him a tall glass half-filled with a pale blue liquid. "Trust me, it'll help."

He took the glass from her and looked from it to
her and back again before taking a cautious sip. It had
a mild, fruity taste and he downed the rest of it
quickly.

"First of all, forget everything they drilled into
you in your lessons," she said, sitting down beside
him. "There's nothing special about us, we are not the
last hope of the Ardraci race. We are just a man and a
woman coming together to create life between us."

She took the empty glass and set it on the table
beside the bed.

"You may not believe it now, but in time you will
come to enjoy the prospect of breeding, maybe even
look forward to it as much as I do." Her hand ghosted up and down his arm in a reassuring caress.

Ravi wasn't sure what to say in response. Her fingers stroking his arm were invoking a strange feeling
inside him. Then the breeding drug kicked in and his
whole body felt like it was on fire.

"My name is Ondine," she told him, still stroking
his arm.

Ravi looked down at her hand, surprised there
were no sparks where she made contact with him. He
could feel his body's response to the powerful breeding drug and it filled him with confusion.

"What are you thinking, Kairavini?"

"Ravi," he said, a little breathlessly. "My friends
called me Ravi. And I'm thinking there must be something wrong with me."

"Why do you think that?"

"I - I - your touch makes me feel . . . I don't think I'm supposed to feel this way."

"I'm going to let you in on a secret, Ravi," Ondine told him, her breath warm on his neck as she whispered close to his ear. "What you're feeling is pleasure, and it's a very natural feeling for what we're about to do."

"It is?" he asked, not quite sure he believed her.

"Yes, let me show you."

The hand stroking his arm moved upwards. Using both hands now, she gently massaged his shoulders, her breasts brushing his arm as she leaned closer. Ravi shuddered in response, feeling his penis growing hard within his drawstring trousers. His breath quickened as she drew back and pulled her tunic over her head. As pale as he was, she was even paler and he was filled with the urge to touch her.

As if divining his thoughts, she took his hand and placed it on her breast. He was mesmerized by her breasts. They were soft and full, tipped with pale pink nipples that contracted tightly at his touch. He cupped the weight of the soft globes in his hands, thumbs stroking her nipples.

"Yes," she hissed, pushing forward into his touch.

Emboldened by her reaction, and fueled by the breeding drug, he stood up and moved her so that she was lying on the bed, removing her trousers as he did so. He swept a hand over her skin.

"You're so soft," he murmured. She looked nothing at all like the illustrations used in the classroom. Her full breasts rose and fell with her rapid breath. She had a narrow waist that flared out into generous hips. Her legs were long and slender and where they met was a thatch of golden curls.

"Touch me," she begged.

Ravi stroked her breasts, cupping them, squeezing them. They felt so good beneath his hands, and given the way Ondine kept pressing them upwards, it must have felt equally good to her having them touched. Why had they never mentioned this in the classes?

"I want to touch you too," she said.

Ravi almost growled as his cock twitched at the idea of her hands on him. Quickly he stripped off his own clothing and lay down beside her. He could see the admiration in her eyes as she looked at his naked body and it filled him with pride. Then she was running her hands over his chest and torso and the tension filling him ratcheted up a notch.

His eyes widened and he jerked as one slender hand wrapped around his cock. "Ondine, I don't think- "

"I'm sorry," she said breathlessly. "I forgot how quick first times can be with the drug. Let me get into position."

This was it. If not for the breeding drug Ravi would have frozen as Ondine wriggled her way into the center of the bed.

"It's all right," she said softly, "You know what to do."

And Ravi found, to his surprise, he did. Raising himself up, he moved until he was between her open legs. Hitching himself upwards a bit, he braced himself on one hand and used the other to guide himself between her glistening folds.

He groaned and closed his eyes as he slid his cock deeper into her hot, wet sheath. His whole body quaked. It made every notion of pleasure he'd ever had pale in comparison. Slowly he pulled back and just as slowly thrust forward again. Ondine moaned beneath him and his eyes snapped open, afraid he was doing something to hurt her. The look of pure bliss on her face reassured him.

As much as he would have loved to have kept up this slow slide in and out, the sensations sparking along the nerve synapses where their bodies met wouldn't allow for it. His strokes became faster, harder, and Ondine rose to meet each thrust. Her legs wrapped around his waist and she slid one hand between them, near to where they were joined.

Ravi had no idea what she was doing, nor did he really care. He was lost in the breeding heat. His world had narrowed to the feel of the woman under him and the tension coiling at the base of his spine. He began to stroke faster. Ondine cried out and jerked beneath him, waves rippling through her snug channel. The sensation was too much for him and he exploded in response, spilling his seed deep within her.

Odine's legs slipped from around his waist and Ravi hung his head, panting for breath. When he was able, he pulled free and then moved to lie beside her on the bed.

"That was . . . marvellous," she said with a sigh of pure satisfaction.

"It was like nothing I ever dreamed of," Ravi told her. "But I do have one question."

"I'd be happy to answer."

He looked over at her with a grin. "Do we have enough time to try it again?"

* * * * *

A breeding took place over the course of five days, two hours each day. By the third day Ravi no longer needed the breeding drug and by the fifth he found himself reluctant to part from Ondine and told her as much.

"In the beginning, so I'm told, the breedings took place for ten consecutive days. But it was found that while ten days of breeding resulted in a higher rate of viable pregnancies, it was also enough time for pairs to form an attachment."

"And so they cut it back to five days."

"Yes. Fewer viable pregnancies, but less risk of attachments being formed."

"Less risk? Or no risk?"

"It was thought to be no risk," she said, "But such things are not always under the purview of science."

"Can I ask you something?"

She smiled at him. "Always with the questions, young Kairavini. What is it this time?"

"Did you ever form an attachment?"

Her smile faded. "Every time," she said quietly. "Do not worry about it," she continued, "such feelings quickly fade and I will only be a pleasant memory by your next breeding."

"I find that hard to believe."

She shrugged. "It's true."

"Will I ever see you again?" he persisted.

"To be sure, my friend. Though with your power level I think it will some time before it is my turn again."

Chapter Six

From Nereida's Journal:

A first breeding goes something like this: The Breeder is given a drug that prepares her body for what is to come. Her hymen has already been broken, under anesthetic during a visit to the infirmary, to ensure her first time is pain free. A carefully selected Seeder is brought to her and the breeding drug is made available to him as well. There is no foreplay, no emotional interaction. They are there for one purpose only, to create a child for the Program. When the Seeder is finished, he disengages and leaves and the Breeder is well taken care of in hopes she's been impregnated.

So that you may understand the vast chasm between Breeders and those with the label of Mistake, I share with you my first time: Mistakes are given no drugs to ease them in the sexual act. The man who came to my door was named Cullen, and I later learned he was the head of security. He had a fondness for deflowering virgins - I was his reward for some service he had done for Dr. Arjun. What I remember most was my fear and the pain, and how much he enjoyed both. When he was finished with me he shoved me aside and told me I'd hardly been worth the effort.

It was, in fact, more than five years before he saw Ondine again. In the meantime Ravi had become used to the breedings, using what he'd learned from her to make it as pleasurable as possible for both parties. Some of the breeders were grateful for this, others were indifferent. One thing Ravi learned was that every Breeder was different, something his instructors had not told them.

"Kairavini!" she exclaimed when he entered the room. "I'm so glad it is to be you for my last breeding."

"Ondine! I'm happy to see you too." He pulled her into his arms for a great hug. "What do you mean this will be your last breeding? Who will teach all the youngsters about pleasure?"

She blushed. "That task will fall to another now. I'm not getting any younger you know, and Dr. Arjun has decided that this will be my last child for the program."

Ravi pulled back to look down at her. "Child?"

Ondine laughed at the expression on his face. "You men are all the same. So concerned with the act that you forget the purpose of our time together."

He looked at her ruefully. "You're right."

It was the one subject that by some unwritten rule none of them ever talked about - offspring. Everyone in the breeding program had a basic knowledge of genetics. It was a well known fact that not every breeding resulted in a pregnancy and not every pregnancy resulted in a child for the program. But it was not something that was ever talked about.

There was a question in his eyes and though she knew she shouldn't, she answered it anyway. "Yes, our first breeding was successful, but I was unable to carry the child to term."

"I'm sorry, I-"

She put her fingers over his lips. "Don't be. It happens from time to time. Obviously it was just a random thing, otherwise I would not be here again. Now, stand back and let me look at you."

He did as she asked, unselfconscious as he pulled off his clothes. Ondine's eyes widened in appreciation. Gone was the awkward, slender youth she had once known. Before her stood a man. He was broader through the shoulders, well-formed muscles filling out what was once just a promise. The hair was a little longer, but the grin on his face was one she remembered. All in all, he'd matured nicely.

"I see you've been making good use of the fitness rooms," she said.

"Had to have some way of getting rid of all that excess energy between breedings."

Ondine laughed. "Come here and let me see if you've remembered what I taught you."

He joined her on the bed. "Maybe this time I can teach you a thing or two."

* * * * *

Ravi paced back and forth in his room. Though he'd thoroughly enjoyed his time with Ondine, it made him sad to realize that the end of their breeding together meant he'd never see her again. Did this mean he'd formed an attachment?

Of course you formed an attachment, Nereida's voice filled his mind. *It would be more unusual if you had not.*

How so? he asked, flopping down on his bed.

She was your first, you were her last. I'm sure you have a special place in her heart as well. But I think that's only to be expected among the Breeders.

But there's been so many years in between, you don't think that's cause for concern? The fact that I feel . . . I'm not sure what I feel beyond this unnatural attachment.

Ravi, you worry needlessly, as always. I don't believe it is the kind of attachment that could bring trouble to you. She's just special, that's all.

What about you? Do you have any among those you're paired with who's special?

There was a long hesitation before she answered. *I have not had as many pairings as you,* she said finally, *but of those, yes, there is one who is . . . special to me.*

Nereida . . .

Yes, brother? she prompted when his thought trailed off.

Do you ever have doubts about the breeding program?

There was a sharp stab of bitterness, quickly cut off. *Yes,* she said. With that her presence in his mind vanished.

Ravi was sorry he'd brought the subject up. Contact between them had become rare over the last few years. He'd thought it was because their lives were so different, but now he wasn't so sure. He remembered what Ondine had said about children - about not carrying his first child to term. Did Nereida have trouble carrying a child to term?

He got up and started pacing again. They weren't supposed to think about things like this. The offspring of these unions were not theirs, they belonged to the program. He shouldn't be thinking about anything beyond fulfilling his duty. He couldn't seem to help himself though. How many breedings had he participated in over the years and how many of them had resulted in a child? Part of him wished he could find out.

Abruptly, he stopped pacing. There *was* a way to find out.

* * * * *

Even though those of the compound had no access to the natural progression of time in the outside, Dr. Arjun kept to a day/night schedule on the inside. Ravi waited, somewhat impatiently, until he was sure everyone was settled for the night and the lights were at half power in the corridors.

With the ease of much practice, he circumvented the lock on his door and stepped out into the corridor. One thing that hadn't changed over his years of breeding, he still liked to wander through the complex at night. Most of the time he spent exploring the tunnels and caverns of the volcano, but he hadn't forgotten how to navigate the rest of the complex.

Security was lax at night, especially in the residential sections. Though the adults were free to come and go at will during the day, within their specific sections, at night the doors to the rooms were locked. After having mastered the lock on the massive door leading to the cave system of the volcano, the lock on his own door was hardly a challenge.

He moved with confidence through the residential section but slowed when he approached the area with the labs. There should be no one working this late at night, unless they were in Dr. Arjun's private

labs and he was not foolish enough to venture in that
direction. Pausing once to duck into an empty room
to avoid a security patrol, he made it safely to the records room.

Once inside it struck him what a daunting task it
was he'd set himself. The room was enormous, row
upon row of files with several tables scattered
throughout for sorting. He'd overheard one of the
technicians complaining about having to make written
reports and learned that Dr. Arjun didn't trust his
computer equipment when it came to storage. They
were old and replacement parts were hard to find, but
it was too dangerous to bring in new equipment. Ravi
had no idea why replacing equipment would be dangerous, but he was just as glad it was. Searching records on the computer would have been impossible
for him.

Using a small, hand-held light he started checking
the labels on the boxes closest to the door, searching
for an index of some kind. He finally found it in a
box on the third shelf from the top. As he started
flipping through the index labels there was a sound at
the door. Quickly turning off his light he moved into
concealment, crouching down beside one of the sorting tables.

The door opened and closed again, the lock
snicking back into place. An indistinct figure made its
way to one of the shelves and pulled out a file box.
Carrying it over to the sorting table closest to the

shelf unit, whoever it was set it down and produced a light of their own.

By their furtive movements, Ravi realized who-ever it was had no more business being in here than he did. Silently he rose to his feet and moved behind them. Using a defensive hold he'd learned but never thought he'd ever use, he secured the intruder in his arms, only then realizing it was a woman.

Chapter Seven

From Nereida's Journal:

It feels somewhat strange writing all of this down, the story of my life, such as it is. But Sta'at says it is important I do so and I have come to trust her judgment in these things. She's not like me, she's an Illezie, the alien race that have been care-takers to the Ardraci since the beginning. I've never seen her, I don't even know for sure that she is a 'her'. I'm not entirely cer-tain the Illezie have genders as we know them. I do know they're very good at dodging questions and the power they show the rest of the universe is just a small portion of what they pos-sess. And I know their names can be incredibly long - they add a syllable for each decade they live. Sta'at's true name is seven-teen syllables.

Taja Windsinger froze as the stranger's arms locked around her. As an Ardraci Black Ops operative, she couldn't afford for her mission to become compromised. Exerting her iron control, she checked her reflexive move to break free, which in all likelihood would result in broken bones. And not her bones.

Several things were immediately apparent to her. Her assailant was a man, well muscled but not heavy set, not too much taller than she was. From the feel of his clothing, he was not a security guard.

"Let go of me," she hissed.

At the sound of her voice, the arms loosened and she was able to pull free. She spun around to face him.

"Who are you?" they asked at the same time.

She snapped on her tiny light. "You're certainly not a guard," she said, playing the light over him. "And you're not dressed like a technician. What business do you have in here?"

"I might ask you the same," he responded. "What business does a security guard have, skulking around the records room?"

He'd be shocked to know the truth, that she'd been sent by the authorities to infiltrate Arjun's operations, a precursor to bringing him down. Her entire team had volunteered for the mission, and it was her skill that secured her place for the initial reconnaissance. The Illezie had connections with the Senisrei mercenaries Arjun used for his security. It had been easy enough to be included amongst them.

"I could just report you and let Dr. Arjun deal with you . . ."

"You could," he agreed, more at ease now. "But you might want to think about the consequences of such an action. The worst that would happen to me would be having my privileges revoked for a period of time. But you? I doubt Dr. Ajrun would take kindly to one of his security officers snooping around."

Whatever else he was, he certainly wasn't lacking in cockiness. "What makes you so sure of yourself?"

"This," he said, holding up the wrist with is designation tattoo.

"You're from the breeding program, aren't you?" she asked. "A Seeder." A slight shiver of revulsion went up her spine.

He cocked a brow and leaned one hip against the table. "And why should it matter what I am?"

"It doesn't," Taja snapped. There was no way she was going to get into an ethical debate with one of the participants of Arjun's breeding program. It was appalling, people allowing themselves to be bred like animals. "What are you doing in here?"

"I was looking for information," he admitted. "And you?"

"The same."

They stared at each other for a moment.

"So now what?" he asked.

Taja hesitated. She should report him, but then she'd have to explain what she was doing in here herself and she couldn't exactly do that. Searching for incriminating information wasn't one of her duties as a mere guard.

"Now you go back to wherever you came from and we'll forget this ever happened."

He shook his head. "I don't think so."

"I beg your pardon?" she looked at him in surprise.

"It's too risky. It's almost time for the guards to patrol the corridors. You wouldn't want me to get caught out of my room after hours, would you?" He flashed a grin at her.

"Look, this isn't some game we're playing here. You -"

They both froze at the sound of movement on the other side of the door.

"This way, hurry." He grabbed her hand and pulled her with him towards the back of the room.

There was a sorting desk at the very back with just enough room for them to both fit under. Unlike the others, this one had a panel along the front that reached almost to the floor. Unless someone came up behind it, they'd never know anyone was concealed under it.

They just ducked under when the records room door was unlocked and opened, and a bank of lights at the front of the room came on.

"I don't see why we have to do this now," a male voice said. "The records aren't going anywhere. Why does Arjun need them in the middle of the night?"

"I don't ask stupid questions, I just obey orders," a second voice said. "That's why I haven't disappeared like all the others."

"Let's just get what we need and get out of here. This place gives me the creeps."

They moved efficiently, going to the proper shelves and pulling out files from boxes. Gathering up a neat stack, they shut off the lights behind them and locked the door once more.

Taja and her companion waited a heartbeat before uncoiling themselves from under the desk.

"What did he mean, about him not disappearing like all the others?"

"You haven't been here long, have you? People who displease Dr. Arjun have a habit of leaving very abruptly."

"Leaving's not the same as disappearing," she said with a frown.

"I've seen it a few times, security escorting people out of the compound."

"Do you think they might be in the city? Or maybe they went off world somewhere?" It could really help their case if they could find some of these people.

He looked at her soberly. "They weren't escorted to the outside; they were being escorted deeper into the volcano."

It took her a moment to process what he was saying. He couldn't possibly be implying what she thought he was, could he? Obviously he was mistaken. There must be a passage through the cave system to the other side of the volcano. And there had to be a map of some kind for that cave system. It was just a matter of finding it.

"We need to leave," he said. "They'll be changing the guard soon and the early guard does a thorough check of the records room."

"How do you know this?" Even she hadn't got the schedule straight yet, and she was working as a guard.

"Years of patient observation," he said with a grin.

Taja wondered just how many years he'd been making these night time forays, and for what purpose. It was on the tip of her tongue to ask before she remembered that she was not here to make conversation, she was here on a mission.

"You feel free to leave," she told him. "I'm going to finish what I came for."

He shook his head. "You don't understand. If Dr. Arjun is working in his secure lab tonight, then that means the two technicians will be back for more information. They never just make one trip. And they'll have Arjun's special security with them."

Taja hesitated. As much as she disliked being told what to do, she suspected he was telling the truth. And if she was caught by Ajun's personal guards her mission would be over before it was even started.

The mission was more than just about bringing Arjun to justice. There were innocent children to think about, products of his insane breeding program. And the location of the facility made it all too easy for Arjun and his followers to escape deeper inside the mountain.

Attempts had been made by a local monastery to navigate the cave system under and through the mountain, but they'd eventually given up. While it was generally agreed there was probably a way through the volcano to the other side, no one was quite sure which passage was the right one.

Her Illezie contact had warned her she'd need every ounce of patience she could muster for this assignment. It was going to be slow going and they needed to be very cautious. They'd also mentioned they were in contact with someone on the inside, and had been for some time. It was how they'd found Arjun in the first place. Could this man be the one?

She studied him surreptitiously. While he seemed sincere in his desire that neither of them get caught, there did not appear to be anything more than that.

Their meeting was just a coincidence, although her sister would have called it fate.

"All right," she said. "Lead the way."

His body blocked her line of vision so she couldn't see exactly what it was he did to get the lock open, but it gave him no trouble at all. They were quiet as they slipped through the door and locked it behind them, and made their way silently through the lab area. The light was at half power but it was more than enough to give Taja a better look at her companion.

He was handsome enough to surprise her. Somehow she'd always thought the people who participated in Arjun's breeding program would be more ordinary looking. Or maybe this one was an exception. Judging by his build and his blonde hair he was a Water Elemental. He moved with the grace of a cat. The view from behind was spectacular.

They reached the main corridor without running into any other guards. There he turned and flashed his grin at her again, as though he knew she'd been admiring him. She scowled back.

"I hope we run into each other again sometime," he said. He was gone before she could form a reply.

Chapter Eight

From Nereida's Journal:

At first Sta'at was just a voice in my head, much like the way Kairavini and I communicate. Her voice sustained me through the worst of tespiro - talking to me, singing to me. Hers was the voice that pulled me back when I was ready to face the darkness. And just before my first time with Cullen I became her Ilarie and we became inseparable. And when I say inseparable, I mean it in every sense of the word. Ilarie means vessel in the Illezie language. I am the vessel that holds the soul of Sta'at. Don't ask me how such a thing is done, I have no idea. And Sta'at is not forthcoming with details. I used to believe my connection with Kairavini meant we were never alone, but there are times when I need to block him from my mind, just as I am sure there are times he blocks me. Some things a brother and sister should not share. But it is different with Sta'at. She is part of me. And it was she who bore the brunt of what Cullen did to my body.

Ravi was fortunate that he didn't run into a security patrol on his way back to his quarters. His mind was on his encounter in the records room, not where he was going. Once he was safely in his room with the door shut, he breathed a sigh of relief.

He'd been utterly shocked when he realized the person he'd held in the records room had been a security guard, and a female one at that. The only time he ever saw a female guard was during a breeding. Just as males were escorted to a breeding by a male guard, females were escorted by a female guard.

This one had been different though. She was small enough to fit comfortably in his arms, and through that little contact he could tell she was in excellent shape. He grinned, remembering the view of her by the half light in the labs. Even the severe uniform couldn't hide her curves. Very excellent shape indeed.

He had to wonder, what kind of information would a security guard be looking for? Records of guards who'd disappeared maybe? The look on her face when he suggested that those who disappeared were taken further into the volcano spoke volumes. First, that she didn't quite believe him, and second, that she was appalled at the thought it might be true.

Flopping onto his back on his bed he stared up at his ceiling. He couldn't get the feel of her in his arms out of his mind. Nor the way they fit so comfortably together when they were forced to hide under the desk. He wished he'd thought to ask her name.

He couldn't wait to see her again.

* * * * *

As the door slid shut behind her, Taja breathed a sigh of relief. She'd made it back to her room with no one even realizing she'd left. In the six weeks she'd been here she still hadn't come up with any ideas on how they could capture Arjun.

Killing him, on the other hand, would be no problem at all. But the Illezie wanted him alive, as did the Ardraci authorities. And since she hadn't reached her high rank in the Ardraci Black Ops by disobeying orders, she would continue to search for a way to bring him to justice.

She stripped off her uniform and did a series of stretches before crawling into bed. Her Illezie mentor wasn't kidding when he told her she'd need every ounce of patience she possessed. Patience was not one of her long suits; she burned with the need to bring Arjun to justice.

Her grandfather Kade had been one of Arjun's followers, back on Ardraci. Illness had kept him from joining the others when they fled the planet. Instead he, and a handful of others who'd been left behind, continued Arjun's teachings in secret. They were not able to continue the breeding experiments, but they were able to perpetuate the ideals of the purity of the Ardraci race - that procreation should take place only within the Elemental groups.

The group was discovered before Taja and her sister Nakeisha were born. None of the rest of the family had known he was a Malcontent. It took a confession from Kade's own lips before their grandmother would believe he was involved - she never got over the disgrace.

When Taja and Nakeisha heard the story as children, they vowed to bring honor back to the family name. Nakeisha had gone on to become a powerful Wind Elemental and mete out justice through diplomatic channels, while Taja honed her skills as a warrior and rose quickly through the ranks of the Ardraci Black Ops, a special force that received training from the Illezie themselves.

And now here she was, chafing at the time it was taking to bring one man to justice. Although it wasn't really one man, was it? There were all the technicians and lab workers, not to mention the adults involved in the breeding program.

That line of thinking brought her around to the man she'd met in the records room. He had a quiet strength, and was undeniably handsome. What was a man like him doing in the breeding program? She could not fathom how anyone would allow themselves to be used in such a way. To be bred like animals, every breeding calculated to bring specific results.

He was nothing like she expected one of them - what were they called, Seeders? He was nothing like she expected a Seeder to be. A shiver went through her as she remembered how perfectly she fit in his arms, and how good those arms felt around her. What had he been looking for in the records room?

Unlike her sister, Taja did not possess the mental acuity to speak with the Illezie mind to mind. Instead she'd been fitted with an ETT, an Esper Thought Transfer device, that would allow her to make brief contact with her mentor. She bit down hard with her back molar to activate the device.

You are late tonight, the voice drifted through her mind.

I'm sorry, it couldn't be helped.

There was a mental sigh. *It never can. What have you to report?*

I was able to access the records room but I had little time to search for a map. There was someone else in there.

Were you seen?

Yes, but it's all right. He wasn't supposed to be in there either - I believe he was one of the Seeders. She was unable to repress the mental revulsion she felt at the name.

You must get over your prejudice, the voice in her head told her. *Things are not always what they seem.*

I - she hesitated, *I wondered if he might be the one who's been in contact with your people.*

No. *He is not.*

W*ouldn't it be better if I made contact with the informant? At the very least they might know where there's a map of this place.*

No.

I*n that case, I have nothing else to report.*

V*ery well. Contact again in two days.*

The presence in her mind vanished.

* * * * *

It had been two weeks since Taja encountered the Seeder in the records room. In that time she had learned a great deal about the program and what she learned confused her.

"Be not so quick to judge," her sister Nakeisha had told her before she left Ardraci. "Things are not always as they appear."

"Is this the ambassador talking, or the sister?" Taja asked.

"It is someone who does not wish you to miss something wonderful because your eyes are closed to the truth."

Taja hated it when her sister came out with cryptic remarks like that, it made her sound like an Illezie, but she had to admit Nakeisha had been right. Things were not as they seemed in the compound. For one thing, she had assumed that everyone, barring the guards, participated in the breeding program.

Instead it was a select group between twenty and thirty years of age.

This week she'd hopefully find out more about them. The duty roister had her on breeding escort, whatever that was. With a sigh she pulled on her uniform and made sure her hair was secure. Time to report to her team leader.

"The task is simple. Here's your list of Breeders." She was handed a data pad. "These are their room numbers, and here are the breeding rooms you will be escorting them to. After their time is up you will escort them back to their rooms."

"I understand," Taja said.

"They are allowed complete privacy for the breeding, but you and the male guard will station yourselves outside the door."

"Understood." It was on the tip of her tongue to ask whether they would be standing guard to keep the Breeders from being disturbed, or to prevent them from leaving the room. Somehow, she felt that the team leader would not appreciate the question.

"There are attendants who oversee the cleaning and supplying of the breeding rooms, but you would be wise to double check to make sure there's a good supply of the breeding drug. It's in a bottle like this." The team leader showed her the dark blue bottle. "Do you have any questions?"

It was on the tip of her tongue to ask what exactly the breeding drug was, but instead Taja answered, "No sir."

"Very well, dismissed."

The first two Breeders she escorted seemed indifferent to what they were about to do. Taja escorted them to their breeding rooms, checked to make sure the dark blue bottle on the table beside the bed was full, and then stood just outside their door. A male guard brought the Seeders, who also seem somewhat indifferent to the whole procedure.

This was nothing like Taja thought it would be. The male guard stationed himself on the opposite side of the door and kept silent vigil with her. When the time was up, they escorted their charges back to their rooms.

The third Breeder Taja escorted seemed in very good spirits, as though this was something to look forward to. Hers was the attitude more in keeping with what Taja expected. It was too bad the Seeder brought to her seemed almost sullen. Taja couldn't help wondering if the Breeder was disappointed.

The final Breeder she was to escort was a whole different story. Taja knocked twice on her door and when there was no answer used her security pass to open the door. She glanced down at the data pad and then called out, "WE-02-77-04, I am here to escort you to your breeding."

The girl gave a sniff and then uncurled herself from where she lay on her bed. "I'm sorry. I must have lost track of the time."

"Are you all right?" Taja asked gently.

"Forgive my weakness," the girl, for she was little more than that, said. "This is my first breeding and I let my fears get the best of me. But I'm ready now. I live to serve."

Taja was torn between wanting to reassure her and just doing her duty. There was no choice really, she was here to do a job. Silently she escorted her charge to the breeding room and made sure there was plenty of the breeding drug. Whatever it was, it could only help the situation.

With a heavy heart she left the girl sitting on the bed and took her station outside the door. The man that was escorted to the room was much older and larger than the girl inside. He was another of the ones who seemed indifferent and Taja could only hope that he'd ease the girl's fears first.

When it was over and the Seeder and his guard had left, Taja entered the room to find the girl curled up on the bed, crying. The bottle with the breeding drug in it lay shattered on the floor.

"What happened?" she asked.

"It-it was my fault," the girl said. "I accidentally knocked the bottle to the floor. He-he-he wouldn't let me ask for another. He said anyone that c-c-clumsy didn't deserve it."

Taja's lips tightened as she fought the urge to run after the men and beat the Seeder to a pulp. This was inexcusable. Instead she contacted the infirmary.

"I need an attendant in breeding room W36."

A medical team arrived quickly. The young Breeder was sedated and taken to the infirmary.

"You'll need to report this," the attendant told Taja. "She's torn up inside and won't be able to be bred again for at least a week, which means it'll be past the prime ovulation period. Dr. Arjun is not going to like this."

Though outwardly stoic, Taja seethed on the inside. It was unconscionable that all she could do was make a report. She hoped the bastard got removed from the breeding program.

When she got back to her quarters after making her report, Taja began to drink. She knew she shouldn't, but for once she was throwing caution to the winds. Ha! Winds. Her sister's winds. Winds that would never be hers.

Suddenly, she couldn't bear the thought of being alone. She poured herself another drink. There was no one here she could talk to. The other guards were taciturn at best. The technicians and lab workers kept to themselves.

Sitting up she had a sudden thought. There was one person she could go to.

Chapter Nine

From Nereida's Journal:

*Something else you should know about me is that I have vis-
ions. It was, in fact, this ability that drew Sta'at to me in the
first place. Even as a child I was able to sometimes "see"
things. Sometimes the visions would seize me when I was
awake, but the more powerful ones came to me in sleep. And so
powerful were these visions that I would sometimes reflect them
outwards. What this usually meant was that everyone in my
dorm would suffer nightmares. But one night the projection was
strong enough that Sta'at felt it, all the way at the outer edge of
our galaxy. She was unable to determine what planet I was on
and could not seek me out physically, so instead made contact
with me mentally and we began forming a bond. Then, after I
passed my tespiro, she sent her consciousness to me and I became her Ilarie, which I will be until we are free of this place
and she can return to her corporeal form. At least that was the*

story she gave me at the time. I have since learned that things are not always as they seem - the Illezie most of all.

A faint noise pulled Ravi's attention away from his computer console. At first he wasn't sure he'd heard anything. Then the noise came again and he realized it came from his door.

Nereida? he asked. She was the only one he could think of who might risk visiting him.

Yes, brother? came the sleepy reply.

I'm sorry, I did not mean to awaken you. I thought - I thought you might have been seeking me out.

Not I, brother dear, she replied, sound much more awake. *I am not the foolish one who wanders at will.* The voice in his mind paused, as though she were listening to something else. *But someone else does. You'd best open the door for her before she changes her mind.*

She? But who? But it was too late, Nereida's voice vanished from his mind.

More curious than ever, Ravi opened his door. The illumination in the corridor was at half power and the light from his room fell onto the security guard he'd run into in the records room, her fist raised to knock again. She blinked in the sudden brightness and he saw that her eyes were grey.

"Oh! I, uh . . . I'm not sure why I'm here," she said, uncertainly. "I'm sorry I bothered you. I should go."

"No, wait!" he said as she turned to leave. "Please, you're not bothering me. Come in."

She hesitated on the threshold. Seeming to make up her mind she slipped inside and the door slid shut behind her. Ravi watched in silence as she made a circuit of his room.

"Are you looking for something?"

"This is your living quarters, isn't it?"

"Ever since I recovered from my *tespiro*," he said, more curious than ever. "And how did you know which room was mine?"

"I remembered your designation from when I had my light on you in the records room and you had your arm up to shield your eyes," she replied absently.

His eyebrows rose in surprise. She was a security guard. Why bother remembering if she wasn't going to report him?

"Where are the mementos?" she asked, genuinely bewildered.

"The what?"

"Childhood mementos. Like books or toys or even photographs?"

"Photographs?"

"Facsimiles of friends or fam-" She broke off whatever she was about to say as she turned to face him. "Never mind. What's your name, anyway?"

"AE-03-"

"No, no, no. Not your designation. I know your designation. Don't you have a name?"

"Kairavini. My name is Kairavini."

"Kairavini." She rolled his name around on her tongue. "It suits you," she said, sitting down on his bed.

There was something about her behavior that was off, beside the fact that she was here in his quarters without any apparent reason. All at once he realized what it was.

"You're intoxicated," he said, not sure whether to be amused or appalled.

Drawing herself up proudly she said, "I am not!" She held the pose for several seconds before slumping back down. "Yes I am. I hope you don't mind."

Ravi grinned at her. "I've read about people being intoxicated before. I've just never seen one."

"You don't drink?"

"Not intoxicants."

"You should try it some time. Why don't you sit down?" She patted a spot on the bed beside her.

Still mystified as to why a security guard would allow herself to become intoxicated and then come seek him out, he sat down. Leaning over, she kissed him on the lips. Ravi pulled back in surprise.

"What are you doing?"

"I should think it's perfectly obvious. I'm kissing you. Once you start kissing me back we'll see where things go."

"I don't understand."

Taja pulled back and took a good look at him. "You really don't understand do you?" She hesitated a moment. "Kairavini, can I ask you something?"

"Of course."

"What exactly happens during a breeding?"

Her question caught him by surprise. "Is that why you are here? You wish to breed with me?" The idea held a certain appeal for him, although it would be an unsanctioned breeding.

Taja's mouth opened and closed several times and her face flamed. "That wasn't--I meant to say--oh, damn!"

She blamed the alcohol, which she never should have started drinking. And she blamed the close prox-imity of the too handsome man beside her. His long hair was pale blonde, and his eyes a brilliant blue, characteristics of his element. She'd always been a sucker for Water Elementals. And Kairavini was lean, yet muscular as well. All sorts of thoughts came un-bidden to her.

"That's not why I asked," she managed to get out, voice an octave higher. What was the matter with her?

He looked at her, genuinely amused now. "What do you think happens? A Breeder and a Seeder are brought together to create a new child for the Pro-gram."

"That's it?"

"What more is there?" At first he seemed puzzled, then the expression on his face cleared. "Ah! I understand. You are confusing a breeding with the human sex act that is rife with emotion. We were warned against this in our lessons."

"You were warned about emotions?" Taja was sure she misunderstood.

"We are taught to divorce ourselves from all emotional investment in the act of procreation."

"You get no pleasure out of it at all?" She couldn't have heard that right, but couldn't seem to help pursuing the point.

"Do you get pleasure out of being a guard?"

"Is that what the breeding is for you, nothing more than a job?"

He shook his head. "It is my duty. It's what I was born for. What all of us here were created for, to further the Program."

Taja looked at the man sitting beside her. She could sense no deception in him. He truly believed what he was saying. "What was it like for you growing up?"

He shrugged. "I stayed in the boys dormitory until I passed my *tespiro*, then I was given this room. We attended classes--"

"What about your parents?"

"My parents?" he asked, brow knitted in a frown. "They, too, were part of the Program. We are taught not to dwell on such things."

"You never knew your parents?" she asked, voice barely above a whisper. "What about your siblings?"

"If I have siblings, they would be part of the Program as well. In different year groups of course."

"Of course," Taja echoed. She tried to imagine what it would have been like to grow up not knowing her sister Nakeisha. The very thought of it was too much for her. Unaccountably, tears filled her eyes. One of them spilled over and tracked down her cheek.

"You weep," Kairavini said, dumbfounded. He caught the tear on his fingertip. "For what reason do you weep?"

"I-I-I don't know. You . . . I have a sister and I can't imagine never having known her. I just --" She shook her head as more tears spilled over.

He didn't say a word, just pulled her into his arms and held her while she cried. The fact that he didn't know what had her so upset just made it that much worse. At this point her tears were as much for him as they were for herself.

It had been too long since she'd felt a man's arms around her and Kairavini's arms felt almost too good. When she cried herself out she pulled away and he let her go immediately.

"Tell me what has upset you so," he said gently.

"It - I -" she sniffed and accepted the tissue he offered her. "I feel so stupid. It's just . . . I pulled guard duty on breedings this week and there was this

one today . . . it was her first time, and she was upset .
. ."

A frown creased his brow. "Was she not given
the breeding drug? It is one of the guards' duties to
make sure there is a supply available. Is this what has
you upset, you forgot to check?"

"No, there was plenty. But the Seeder was impatient and the bottle was accidentally broken."

"I have heard . . . " he hesitated. "It sometimes
happens with older Seeders, especially when it has
been a long time between breedings, that they become impatient."

"I had to call the medics for her," Taja whispered.

"Ah." He nodded in understanding. "No matter
how impatient a Seeder is, damage to a Breeder is
sheer stupidity. Did you report him to Dr. Arjun?"

"Yes." She paused for a moment then added in a
whisper, "How will she ever get over something like
this?"

"The medical staff will see to it that she is fully
healed before her next breeding."

She looked askance at him. "That's not what I
meant!"

He looked back at her, clearly puzzled. "She will
not be punished, if that is what you fear. It was not
her fault the breeding was unsuccessful."

"The poor girl was brutalized! Of course her body
will heal, but what about her mind? How is she supposed to get over something like this?"

"It is her duty," he said, as though that was the answer to everything.

She stared at him, appalled. "I don't understand you. How can you be so cold?"

"I do not understand you, either," he said. "We exist for one purpose, to further the breeding program. She knows that as well as any one of us. The medics will see to it themselves she's given the breeding drug next time."

Taja tried to imagine what it was like for him, growing up. Never knowing the love of his parents or siblings, never knowing freedom, only knowing this cold sterile world of his. Suddenly, she was unaccountably depressed.

"It's late," she said. "I should go."

Kairavini got up from the bed with her and walked her to the door. She thought he was about to say something else, but evidently changed his mind.

"Thank you for listening to me," she said.

He shrugged his shoulders. "I enjoyed the company. I do not often receive visitors," he added with a ghost of a grin. "Wait," he called as she checked the corridors. "You haven't told me your name."

"Taja," she told him as she slipped out the door. "My name is Taja."

Chapter Ten

From Nereida's Journal:

Ravi, of course, knew about my visions. How could he not, joined as we were, mind-to-mind? As I grew older the visions became stronger and began taking a toll on me, but by this time I had Sta'at to help me hide from Ravi how weak the visions made me. I'm not sure what I thought he would do if he knew - something foolish, I'm sure. Tespiro seemed to be a catalyst for me. Before tespiro most of my visions were half-formed, hard to interpret. The only clear one I can recall is of my mother giving birth to a baby girl, the bittersweet smile on her face as she handed the baby to the mid-wife who spirited her away to be raised elsewhere, and my mother returning to her element. But although after tespiro the visions became clearer, that didn't mean I always knew what they meant. Like my vision of the volcano. It was clear it was going to erupt, but not when or what was going to set it off. I can clearly see the man standing

in the fire, but there's also a woman who's face seems so famili-
ar . . .

Dr. Arjun drummed his fingers on the desk as he
read the report from the infirmary. WE-02-77-04 was
second generation and already a power level 4 - he
hoped that idiot Seeder hadn't ruined her for further
breedings. Damina, the psychologist, recommended
the girl be double-dosed for her next breeding attempt. It galled him that such precautions were necessary. It was just as well the Seeder was nearing the end
of his usefulness - it made the decision to dispose of
him that much easier.

The next report caused the frown on his face to
deepen. The rate of viable pregnancies was steadily
dropping and nothing they did seemed to make a difference. Boosting the Breeder's fertility only resulted
in multiple fetuses, which of course had to be abor-
ted. He'd even tried in vitro procedures but the im-
plants failed seven out of nine times. It was time for
something drastic.

"Cullen, report to my office," he barked into the
intercom, "and bring Damina and Severn with you."

Both Damina and Severn had been with Uri Arjun from the beginning. Damina as both head psychologist and chief medical officer, and Severn as the
chief geneticist. Chatter in the infirmary died instantly
when Cullen appeared in the doorway seeking them

out. Far from being intimidated, however, the pair were slightly annoyed at having their work interrupted with the summons to Arjun's office. As soon as the door shut behind them the chatter started up again, punctuated by more than one breath of relief.

"Be seated, both of you," Arjun directed the pair when they reached his office.

If either of them were surprised by the invitation to sit, they didn't let it show. They both knew from experience that Dr. Arjun preferred to keep visitors standing, all the better to try and intimidate them.

"Cullen, I'd like you to take care of this and then report back to me." Dr. Arjun passed him the file on the Seeder.

"Yes sir." Cullen saluted smartly and left.

"Severn, are you any closer to uncovering the reason for the drop in viable pregnancies?"

"It is as we feared. I've traced the problem back to the isolation of the dominant elemental genes. We discussed this possibility at the outset of the program and it appears our fears are being realized. A viable elemental fetus must contain all four genes, not just the dominant one. We cannot create a pure, singular Elemental."

"And yet the power ratings keep increasing. How do you explain that?"

"You'll note that the higher power ratings have resulted from those who have the higher traces of each element. But our biggest problem is we need a

new infusion of genetic material. I warned you when
we landed here that we didn't have a broad enough
gene pool to complete our work."

Dr. Arjun nodded thoughtfully. "What if I told
you I could get a hold of a new infusion of genetic
material?"

Severn snorted. "I'd say you've been working too
hard. Even if you were able to get a message out
you'd never be able to get anyone from Ardraci here
without the Illezie finding out."

"What if they were already here? At least twenty
possible candidates."

"Then I'd say you were a genius!"

"Damina," Arjun turned to her next. "What kind
of psychological problems would we have to deal
with, bringing a group of outsiders into the fold?"

"Well," she hesitated slightly. "For the group
coming in we could expect hysteria, anger, fear -
nothing that couldn't be overcome by training and
drugs. What ages are we talking about here?"

"I would say half of them will be pre-*tespiro*, the
rest somewhat older." He shrugged, not really caring
beyond the fact that most of them would be of breeding age.

"I dare say the older the participant, the harder it
will be for the adjustment. And we have our own
people to deal with as well. If the outsiders are resist-
ant . . . our people aren't equipped to deal with resistance. They'll have a difficult time understanding it."

"Hmm." Dr. Arjun rubbed his chin with his hand. "But it is doable?"

"Yes, I think it could work. But where are these outsiders coming from?"

"Do either of you remember a midwife named Wynne Ignitus?"

"I do," Severn nodded. "She was Fire, but her gift wasn't strong enough to warrant including her in the program."

"I remember her too," Damina said slowly. "In fact I came to you twice with misgivings about her loyalty to the cause, and both times you dismissed me out of hand."

"It appears you were right about her," Dr. Arjun said mildly, not appreciating the reminder of past mistakes. "Over the course of several years she was smuggling babies out of the old compound. And when we made ready to move, she and several other traitors stole several more children. They have been living in an isolated village all these years."

Severn brightened immediately. "This could be the answer to all our problems!"

Damina was somewhat more cautious in her enthusiasm. "This will have to be handled with care. I've been working on a cognitive inhibitor - perhaps I could modify it to make these newcomers more . . . amenable to their participation in the program."

"That would be excellent. I knew you wouldn't let me down." He beamed at them both, an expression that few staff members ever saw. "I'll make the arrangements to have our stray lambs brought back to the fold at once. I think our meeting here is done, unless either of you have anything to add?"

They were hardly aware of being dismissed, both wrapped up in their thoughts of the work ahead.

Cullen was waiting outside the door and slipped inside as the two left. "The Seeder is being escorted to the disposal area."

"Were there any difficulties?"

"No sir."

"Cullen, my friend." Dr. Arjun was wearing a pleased expression that would have struck fear into many of his subordinates. "The time has come for Project Retrieval. Please make the necessary arrangements."

"Right away, doctor."

* * * * *

Taja was filled with recriminations. She should never have gone to Kairavini's quarters. It was a stupid thing to do, as was her fleeting attempt to seduce him. What had she been thinking?

She cringed when she thought of his reaction to her kiss. His surprise had been so palpable. It was like he'd never been kissed before. But that wasn't possible . . . was it?

When she went over all the things he'd told her she became more confused than ever. She'd been so sure of herself when she got here, so strong in her beliefs. Now she didn't know what to think. The participants in the breeding program weren't the villains she'd thought them to be, they were victims and they didn't even realize it. Their lives had been stolen from them and they'd been brainwashed to believe it was normal.

As she fell asleep she thought of Kairavini's arms, and how good they'd felt around her. What would they feel like if he was holding her with passion, instead of comfort? She had to find some way to help him.

Two days later she escorted another new Breeder to a breeding room. This one was a little more stoic than the last one, but she was still visibly nervous. Taja wished there was some way of reassuring her but to do so would break her cover.

She waited patiently outside the room and only the widening of her eyes gave away the fact that she recognized the Seeder who was escorted in. Kairavini's eyes flickered towards her and he had the audacity to wink at her before the door closed behind him.

Restlessly, she stood guard with her male counterpart. Her thoughts strayed to what was going on in the room behind her. Was he taking his time and soothing the Breeder's fears? Or was he indifferent,

just doing his job with no care to what she was feeling.

But by his own admission, feelings didn't enter
into it. Taja suppressed a shudder. They were no better than animals fulfilling a biological urge. Rutting in
heat. Still . . . there was a part of her that couldn't help
but wonder what kind of a lover he was.

When the allotted time was up, she stumbled as
he came out the door and fell against him. "Sorry,"
she muttered, pressing a data cube into his hand. His
fingers closed around it automatically.

"No harm done," he said, and went docilely with
his escort.

* * * * *

Ravi's breathing was rapid and he was covered in
a fine sheen of sweat. He took a gulp from a glass of
ice water but it did nothing to relieve the burning inside him. Popping the data cube out of the reader, he
held it tight in his hand.

*You are very agitated tonight, brother, is something the
matter?*

No - yes - no.

Amusement filled Nereida's mind voice. *Well
which is it? Yes or no?*

I'm sorry. He ran a hand through his hair. *I don't
know what's the matter with me. I had an . . . encounter with
one of the guards and it's left me very confused.*

Tell me about it, Nereida told him, remembering the night he woke her up by mistake.

Ravi hesitated only a moment, then told her about running into Taja in the records room and her subsequent visit to his room several days later, finishing with the data cube she passed to him after his breeding two days ago.

I *like her. You need to help her however you can,* Nereida said firmly.

What? Whatever Ravi had been expecting her to say, this wasn't it.

She obviously came here for some special purpose and I believe it is for the greater good.

What greater good? he asked, thoroughly confused.

What was on the data cube she gave you?

He squirmed a little, hand tightening around it. *Stories.*

What kind of stories?

With a sigh, Ravi confessed. *At first they were just stories of the outside - far away places, worlds, oceans, planets . . . it sounds wonderful.*

And then? Nereida prompted.

And then the stories became more . . . personal. Stories of men and women together, doing things that would not be sanctioned by the Program.

And how did those stories make you feel?

They - I - you are my sister! I'm not discussing this with you!

He could picture her in her room, grinning at him.

You enjoyed them, didn't you?

Nereida! Ravi's face flamed as he thought of those stories and his reaction to them.

All right, all right, I'll stop teasing.

Why would she give me such things to read?

Maybe she likes you.

What?

Maybe she'd like to do some of those things with you.

Ravi remembered Taja's lips on his - kissing, she called it - and how good it felt. He'd like to try kissing again. If he were honest with himself he'd like to try a great many of the things he read about.

How can I find out what she wants to do?

Well, to begin with why don't you visit her in her quarters? You'll know when you show up at her door whether she wants you there or not.

You mean . . . just go there?

Honestly Ravi, I don't remember you being this slow in school. Just take the data cube back to her if you need an excuse.

Have you 'seen' something? he asked suddenly. *Something concerning Taja and I?*

Ravi . . .

Nereida, tell me!

I see only snatches of what is to come. I still see fire . . . and I see you and a woman who is very familiar, but she is not the one for you. She belongs to the man in the fire. But there is another woman - you are meant to be together. I see you working with her to get people to safety, but the people are strangers.

That's not possible, Ravi replied, his mind's voice a mere whisper.

The fire is coming, Nereida said, no doubt in her mind's voice, *there is no stopping it. As for the rest . . .* she gave a mental shrug. *That will be up to you and her.*

Chapter Eleven

From Nereida's Journal:

Sta'at tells me that this journal will one day become important to my brother Ravi. Lest you think my life was utter misery, dear brother, let me tell you of my beloved Kaine. You will wonder why I did not tell you of him before, especially when I encouraged you in your relationship with Taja. I thought to, at first, to share my happiness. But I feared you would not understand. And then later I realized I could not share my joy without first sharing my sorrow, and my shame. And that, I realized, I must keep to myself. For your sake.

To my great relief, I was not often sought out by the guards. All but a few preferred their woman to be more robust. I had never fully regained the weight I had lost during tespiro and the visions kept me somewhat frail. But there were a few, like Cullen, who received their pleasure through the torment of others. It

was after an encounter with one such as that that I first met
Kaine.

Taja paced inside her room. What had she been
thinking, slipping Kairavini that data cube? All he
needed to do was turn the cube in and if it were
traced back to her that would be the end of her mission. All that work for nothing - except to alert Dr.
Arjun that the Illezie were closing in on him.

She couldn't believe she was foolish enough to
jeopardize the entire mission for . . . what, an attempt
to show a Seeder that what he was missing? To prove
to him that the whole breeding program was unnatural? And why did he matter so much to her?

Checking her time piece she saw that she still had
a few minutes before she was to make her report. She
needed to marshal her thoughts. At least this time she
had something useful to report. Sitting down on her
bed, she tried to push Kairavini out of her mind.

Did he read the stories on the data cube? She
couldn't help but wonder what he thought of them.
Maybe he learned some new techniques to try at his
next breeding. Or perhaps he was appalled and destroyed the cube. How was it possible she was devel-
oping feelings for him? She was Taja Windsinger,
dubbed the Ardraci Ice Queen by her Black Ops team
mates. Oh, how they'd laugh to see her all twisted up
like this over a man!

A chime sounded on her time piece and she bit down to activate the ETT.

Report, her contact said, wasting no time on pleasantries.

There was a request for volunteers amongst the guards for a special assignment. I was not chosen but I overheard two guards that were discussing it. Dr. Arjun is going to be bringing in a new infusion of genetic material for his breeding program. The volunteer squadron is to leave tomorrow.

What form is this genetic material to take?

Children. The guards are being sent after Ardraci children who were raised elsewhere on this planet.

How long before the children are brought into the compound?

The guards are going to have to travel overland by horse so it will take at least a week, maybe two.

I'll inform the council. A ship will be dispatched at once. Is there anything else?

No sir.

Keep us informed if there are any new developments.

The presence in her mind vanished before Taja could reply. She heaved a sigh. What had she expected, a show of curiosity as to how these children were raised outside the compound?

The Illezie she reported to on this assignment was new to her - she didn't even know his name. She missed her regular partner, Dah'mat, as she liked to be called. Taja only tried to pronounce her real name once. After making it as far as the thirteenth syllable, she gave up, much to Dah'mat's relief. Illezie names generally had twelve syllables or more. Rumour had it that a syllable was added for every decade an Illezie lived and it was only after twelve decades they left their home world to mingle with other races.

Dah'mat would have known what to do about Kairavini. At the very least she would have been someone Taja could talk to during her down time. Great care was taken when partnering an Illezie with an Ardraci. There had to be a certain level of respect as well as kinship and above all, trust.

When Taja reached the age where the choice is given each Ardraci to develop their elemental power or give it up, Dah'mat was the one who encouraged her to undergo the *desmirha,* the suppression of the gift, since Taja's lack of ability was only making her miserable. She was also the one who encouraged Taja to join the Black Ops, suggesting that it was the safest outlet for her aggressive nature.

She would be the first to laugh at her for fixating on a man who didn't even know what a kiss was, Taja admitted to herself with another sigh. Dah'mat was never one to let an opportunity to tease pass her by.

It was just as well that breedings were temporarily suspended while the special assignment was taking place. The chances were slim that she'd run into Kairavini in the course of her other duties. She wouldn't know what to say to him if she did.

Maybe some meditation would help. Sitting cross-legged on her bed, she straightened her back and closed her eyes. Her thoughts kept racing through her head like rodents in a maze. Taking a deep breath, she held it in for several seconds and then let it out slowly. Inhale. Exhale. Again.

It was working. She felt calmer already. Another inhale and a frown crossed her face. It was bad enough she couldn't get him out of her mind, now she was breathing in a faint, musky scent that reminded her of him.

Taja's eyes snapped open.

"What are you doing here?"

Kairavini looked at her a little shamefacedly. "I'm sorry, I should have knocked but there was someone coming and I needed to get out of the corridor."

"How did you even get in here? That door was locked."

"I, uh . . . I have a talent with locks."

"That's some talent," she muttered, remembering how easily he'd dealt with the lock in the records room. "Now that you're here, you might as well have a seat."

She found it interesting that he chose to sit in the chair instead of beside her on the bed. "So, Kairavini --"

"Ravi," he said.

"I beg your pardon?"

"I'd prefer it if you'd call me Ravi. That's what my friends called me."

"So you do have friends. I'd wondered about that considered how isolated everyone seems."

"Did have," he corrected, relaxing in his chair a little. "I had friends among my year group when we were still in the dormitory. After we passed our *tespiro* we were given our own rooms but we still shared classes and the common room. It was only after we became Seeders that our duties prevented us from seeking out friendships."

"And you've never snuck out in the night to visit a friend?" Taja asked, genuinely curious.

"A few times," he admitted. "But Zephryn's place in the Program is not as secure as mine and he worried about having an unsanctioned visitor. I haven't seen him in years."

"I'm sorry," she said. "Your lives must be very lonely."

"You get used to it," he said with a shrug.

It was on the tip of her tongue to tell him he shouldn't have to get used to it, but she stopped herself. Instead she asked, "You said your friend's place wasn't as secure as yours, what did you mean by that?"

"Zeph was only a level four Wind, and I'm a level seven Water." When he saw she didn't understand the significance, he went on to explain. "The higher your rating, the more secure your position."

"I see," Taja said thoughtfully. There was no such rating system on Ardraci. An Elemental was judged on their ability and control of their element. "I'm surprised there isn't more of a show of elemental power in the compound."

"I'm not sure I know what you mean."

He looked so guileless sitting there, could he really not know what the ratings meant? "You're a Water Elemental, isn't that right?"

He nodded.

"Have you never been tempted to call up your element, even for fun?"

Shaking his head he said, "What would be the point? My elemental gift is insignificant. When we were taught to use them we were taken to a special place where our gifts were augmented so that we could see what it was like to be a true Elemental."

"But--" she stared at him, shocked. Did he truly not realize that his power rating and his elemental gift were the same thing? How was this possible? Her eyes were drawn to the wide cuff on his wrist. "Ravi," she asked slowly. "You seem to be the only one in the Program wearing a cuff like that. Why is that?"

"This?" He held up his wrist. "After I went through my *tespiro* I had terrible headaches. This has a pain inhibitor in it."

"May I see it?"

When he answered in the affirmative, Taja picked up a micro scanner from the table beside her and went over to him. Waving the scanner slowly over the cuff, she had a sinking feeling she knew what she was going to find. The readings confirmed it.

"What are you doing?" he asked curiously.

"Trying to see what this is made of," she said absently. "Maybe it can help others who suffer headaches." It wasn't quite a lie. If it actually had been a pain inhibitor, it would have been of great value. But pain wasn't what the device inhibited. "It's an ingenious device," she said. Created by an ingenious madman.

"It saved my life, so I'm told."

"And you believe everything you're told by Dr. Arjun?"

"Why wouldn't I?"

Why indeed.

Taja took Ravi's wrist in her hands, turning it back and forth to try and figure out how the device encasing it could be removed. There, a tiny keyhole, easy to overlook.

"I enjoyed the stories on the data crystal you gave me," he said abruptly.

She dropped his wrist and drew back quickly. "You did?" Why did the mere thought of him reading those stories make her breath quicken?

"There were some things I did not understand. I was hoping, perhaps, that you could explain them to me."

"Me?" Taja squeaked.

"I have no one else."

Oh gods and goddesses, what had she gotten herself into? "I'll do my best," she told him. It was the least she could do. After all, she was the one who gave him that data crystal.

"Some of what I read conflicts with what we were taught . . . the emotional aspects, for instance."

Emotional aspects. Right. She could talk about emotions. "You said before you were taught to divorce yourself from the emotional aspects of . . . what you do."

He nodded. "Yes. At the time my friend and I believed it was to keep us from forming attachments to our breeding partners, and what I have read seems to confirm this. In fact, in direct conflict to what we were taught, it appears that the objective of intercourse is to find someone to form an attachment with and procreate only with them."

"It's called falling in love," Taja said softly.

Ravi shook his head. "It is very confusing."

"I'm sorry. It wasn't my intention to make you confused or troubled. Maybe you should just forget about the stories on the crystal."

"I do not want to," he said. "I find myself drawn to these stories of emotional attachment. I wonder what it would be like to feel these things."

"After all these breedings," and she really didn't want to know how many, "have you never felt an attachment to one of your partners?"

"Such things are forbidden."

"That's not what I asked," she said.

Ravi sighed. "My very first. Her name was Ondine, and she told me that forming even a small attachment to a breeding partner makes the breeding easier."

"And was she right?"

He hung his head, as though ashamed. "Yes."

Taja's heart went out to him as she blinked back tears. "Ravi, please listen to me. There is no shame in feeling something for another person. The shame lies with those who have reduced what can be a beautiful thing to something sterile and clinical."

"Why did you give me the data crystal?"

"I don't know." She couldn't quite bring herself to regret it, not if it had him questioning his place in the breeding program. "I guess to give you a glimpse of what life is like beyond this compound."

"But why?" he persisted, looking across the room at her. "There is no outside for us. There is only life in the compound and our participation in the Program."

Again she had to stop herself from saying what she really felt. That what was happening in this compound was wrong. That life should be lived the way it was in the stories on the crystal, not by the dictates of a mad man.

"I'm sorry," she said again. "I should never have given you that crystal."

"I am not sorry," he said, getting up and joining her on the bed. "I enjoyed the stories a great deal. I learned many things from them, it is just unfortunate I cannot use them in a breeding."

"What kinds of things?" she asked, in spite of herself. Her face flamed and she immediately wanted to take the words back.

"This, for instance." He leaned closer and his lips met hers. "I believe you called it kissing," he said, pulling back again.

"Yes," she said, a little breathlessly.

"I understand it gets better with practice." This time he put his arms around her and drew her closer. She went willingly.

The touch of his lips was at first tentative, growing bolder as she showed no signs of resistance. Taja's hands slid upwards to tangle in his hair as she returned his kiss. When they finally broke apart they were both breathing heavily.

"Wow," she said. "I thought you'd never done this before."

"I'm a fast learner," he said with a grin.

Taja's heart rate and breathing were accelerated and she could tell his was as well. Fast learner indeed. There were a thousand questions in his eyes, but as he opened his mouth to speak a chime sounded. She put her hand to his mouth to keep him quiet.

"Yes Captain?"

"Report to the Ready Room."

"Yes sir!"

* * * * *

On impulse, Ravi kissed the palm of her hand. She snatched it away, but he couldn't help noticing she was looking as flushed as he felt. Had she enjoyed the kissing as much as he had?

"I have to go," she said.

There was a hitch in her breath. Was it regret or relief? He was too unsure of himself to ask. Instead, he nodded.

With the fluid grace he'd come to associate with her, she rose from the bed and went to the door. Pausing for a moment she turned back to look at him, all business. "Stay here for a few minutes before following. I wouldn't want to you get caught."

"I'm not sorry I came here tonight," he called after her.

As the door started to slid shut behind her, her words floated back to him, "Neither am I."

Ravi couldn't help the grin that slid across his face. It was really too bad they'd been interrupted, he had many more questions. The kissing had been every bit as pleasurable as the stories had him believing it to be. Would the other things he'd read about in the stories be pleasurable as well? It was hard to believe *anything* could be as enjoyable as kissing.

He was glad the breedings had been temporarily cancelled. It was going to be difficult to do his duty without wanting to try some of the things he'd read about. Sighing, he wished Taja hadn't been called away. He prowled through her room, curious to learn more about her. She was more than just a guard, that much was obvious, but what was she here for?

She seemed to have a great many weapons, but perhaps all guards had such collections. He knew next to nothing about weapons, although several of the boys he'd grown up with had done independent studies about them. They had been forbidden to set up a room where they could practice, and the weapons study had soon been abandoned.

On the small table near her bed she had two photographs. One was of Taja when she was much younger, along with a girl who looked very much like her - likely the sister she had mentioned. They were both smiling; light was falling on them from above and they were standing in a wide, empty space with a carpet of green under their bare feet.

The second picture was of the sister without Taja, but included a man who was resting a hand rather possessively on the sister's shoulder. They each held an infant and were beaming with pride - obviously the infants were their offspring. Curiously, the sister's hair had turned white, the same color as the man's.

He lingered for a moment on the picture. What would it be like to breed with only one woman, to be

there when she had his child? He shook his head ruefully and set the picture down carefully. It didn't matter. His duty was to the Program . . . wasn't it?

The picture, however, served to remind him that
he never did find out about his offspring, the task that
had been interrupted the night he met Taja. Since she
had been called away, there was no reason he couldn't
complete the task now. He had to pass the labs with
the records room on his way back to his quarters anyway, he might as well look up the information.

Chapter Twelve

From Nereida's Journal:

Kaine is from a world very far from here. His race is empathic. He told me later that he could feel my pain from the moment he stepped into the compound. The first few times we were together all we did was talk. I could scarce believe this man wanted nothing more from me than my company. He was so kind to me, his manner so gentle, that it was not long before I craved more from him than just his kind words. I am not ashamed to admit my desire for Kaine. Our first time together was how it should be between a man and woman. Not the cold, emotionless breedings forced upon those in the Program, nor the frantic, un-fulfilling couplings forced upon the M-class. Kaine filled a void inside me that I had not known existed. If I have but one wish, it would be that my brother is freed from this place and that he, too, finds such happiness as mine. No matter how briefly.

Ravi frowned and sat back in the chair he'd pulled up to the sorting table in the records room. He was at the table in the back, with a clear view of the door so he'd have plenty of time to hide should there be a need.

He'd checked his records but could make little sense of the graphs and numbers. Wishing he'd paid closer attention to the classes in genetics and biology, he checked for any notations or summaries, but there was nothing. Maybe such things were kept in a different place. Or perhaps records of offspring were kept in the Breeders files, not the Seeders.

Carefully replacing his file back where it belonged, he tried to remember Ondine's designation. Maybe he'd have more luck with her file. Was it AE-02-49-03, or AE-02-39-04? He checked both records and it was the latter.

Leafing through the charts and graphs in her file, he finally came to the pages in the back that appeared to be a record of the results of her breedings. It was a series of numbers and symbols that made no sense to him. Staring at it, he tried to decipher the meaning. There were two different symbols, one that appeared only twice in the whole record, and a second one that was always followed by a number. What could it mean?

His mind drifted back to the last conversation he'd had with Ondine. She'd been regretful that she hadn't carried his child to term. Ravi's eyes widened in

horror. He'd figured it out. All those numbers. The
symbol meant a miscarriage - the number was how far
along she'd been. Poor Ondine! He hoped with all his
heart that their final breeding had resulted in a child,
not for Dr. Arjun, but for her.

At the very bottom of the record was a completely different symbol in red.

Ravi stared at the symbol stamped on the last
page of Ondine's file. What did it mean? Maybe Taja
would know. Carefully, he detached the page from
the rest of the file and folded it up. Returning the
folder to where it belonged, he hesitated, then pulled
another at random.

Again he saw the same two symbols, although
this time there were four of the first symbol as well as
several of the symbol that was followed by numbers.
He checked another, then another, and the results
were similar. Only a few of the first symbol, but always several of the second followed by the numbers.
Two of the files had only the second symbol followed
by the number, although the list only trailed half-way
down the page before the larger, red symbol was
stamped on it. Altogether five of the ten files he
checked ended with the red symbol.

It was wrong, he knew it was wrong, but he had
to find out. The files were in order by element and
designation. He checked twice in the section for Water but could not find Nereida's file. Frowning, he

realized there were no M designations amongst the breeding files. Why would they be kept separate?

Kairavini, what are you doing?

He started, dropping his light. *What are* you *doing?* he countered, taking a few deep breaths to bring his heart rate back to normal. *Shouldn't you be sleeping?*

I'm a light sleeper and you were thinking too hard, Nereida told him. *Where are you, and what has you so upset?*

I'm not upset, just . . . unsettled. I'm in the records room, he replied, stooping down to retrieve his light.

You know I can sense your emotions as well as your thoughts. What are you looking for that has you so disturbed?

Ravi sighed mentally. *It was foolish, really. I was just checking . . . I wanted to know . . . there was a Breeder . . . I just wanted to see if one of my breedings had been successful.*

There was silence.

Now I've shocked you with the truth, your brother is a deviant.

Oh, Ravi! Of course you're not a deviant. What's deviant is the way we're trained to not care about the results of the breedings.

Now you sound like Taja, he grumbled.

You have seen her again?

Yes. I went to her room tonight, but she got called away.

And now you are restless and looking for trouble to get into.

Though her tone was teasing, Ravi knew she worried about him. *I just remembered that I never finished what*

I started the night I met Taja. I wanted to know if my last breeding with Ondine had been successful.

Ondine? You exchanged names with a Breeder? Do you not realize how dangerous that is?

It wasn't like that! I told you about her. She was my first . . . and I was her last. And I found a symbol in her file I do not understand. So I checked other files and the symbol appears in some of them as well.

I'm sorry, I cannot help you brother. Genetics and biology were not among the things I liked to study.

Ravi made sure the files he'd looked at were returned to their proper places and did a quick check to make sure nothing else was out of place. It was getting late and he should be returning to his room.

I'm hoping that maybe Taja can tell me what the symbol means.

Even though she's just a guard?

Ravi wrestled with his conscience and then confessed, *She is more than just a guard. I believe she's here for another purpose.*

Kiaravini, Nereida's mind voice came slowly. *I've had another vision of the fire, and you and a woman helping others escape the compound. I have a strong feeling that this Taja of yours is the one in my vision. Whatever her purpose is here, you must help her.*

Help her? Help her with what? You don't know for sure there will be a fire --"

Yes I do. And it will be sooner than we realize. Our whole world is about to change.

M*y world is already changing.* Ravi felt weighted down with changes. *I'm starting to question my place in the Program, I'm displaying deviant curiosity about the results of my breedings, and I have thoughts that are unworthy of a Seeder.*

In one of those rare moments of connection he could almost picture her curled up on the bed as she projected a gusty sigh at him.

I*t is only going to get worse for you I fear. But you are not alone. You have me. And, I think, you have Taja as well. Trust her. Help her.*

I*'m just a Seeder. I belong to the Program and nowhere else. I'm no hero to be helping anyone.*

Y*ou are more powerful than you realize,* Nereida told him.

Ravi shook his head as though she could see him as he unlocked the door and shut it firmly behind him so the lock would engage automatically. *I'm just a Seeder,* he repeated.

* * * * *

Taja ghosted along the half-lit corridor, the black of her uniform blending in perfectly with the shadows. She reached the heavy metal security door and paused. Was that the noise of someone approaching?

A whisper of movement was all the warning she had before strong arms locked around her, a hand over her mouth to prevent her from crying out. Before she could strike back she was spun around and a pair of warm lips replaced the hand.

"Kairavini!" she gasped, breaking free from the kiss. "That was a stupid thing to do!"

"You think my kisses are stupid?" he asked, pulling back. "Oh." He suddenly became aware of the wicked knife being held to his throat. "I guess sneaking up on a trained guard isn't the smartest thing I've done in a while."

Taja slipped the knife back into a wrist sheath and took a step back. Her heart was pounding, but she was unwilling to admit it was more than just an adrenalin rush.

"Are all guards armed with those?"

"No," she said with a sigh. "Look, we need to get out of this corridor before someone sees us."

It had been two nights since their last encounter. She'd returned to her quarters after her shift tonight and found a note from Ravi, folded in the shape of a bird, placed neatly on the center of her bed. There was too much activity to meet in either her room or his, but he said he'd be waiting for her in the corridor near the heavy security door that barred them from the rest of the mountain.

He cocked his head to gauge her mood, then suddenly grinned. "I know just the place."

Before she could ask what he was up to, he had the security door unlocked and was holding it open for her.

"How did you do that?" She'd been working on that door for weeks without any luck.

Ravi winked. "Years of practice."

They slipped through the door and the lock engaged automatically when it shut behind them. Taja's eyes widened. When she first arrived she'd been able to confirm what they'd already suspected, that what they saw of the compound from the outside was just a fraction of its true size. All of the living quarters and most of the laboratories were carved from the side of the mountain. And now, beyond this almost impenetrable security door, was evidence they were also making use of the natural cave system of the volcano.

Before them was a large cavern. The floor had been smoothed flat, but there were still stalactites hanging from the ceiling. Wooden crates were stacked neatly on either side of the wide space, the markings indicating they held clothing and supplies. There were several openings in front of them, passageways that led further into the volcano. The lighting here was even dimmer than the half power of the corridors in the compound.

"This way," Ravi told her, tugging her by the hand.

He led her towards the second tunnel from the right, the light just barely bright enough to see by. There were several tunnels leading away from the one they were in, some with lights, some without. Pausing before one of the dark openings, Ravi flicked on a hand held light before leading her onwards. The path twisted and turned for several feet, then narrowed before opening into a small room-like dead end.

"The tunnels in this section are used mostly for storage. This one was rejected because of the way it narrows."

"How did you find this place?"

He shrugged. "I've always like to explore. I almost got caught by a work crew one time and had to hide quickly - the openings without any light are usually a good place to hide because no light means they've been abandoned."

Part of her marveled at his ingenuity, but another part of her wanted to chide him for his rashness. "Just how much of the cave system have you explored?"

"Not as much as I'd like." Ravi sat down and patted the ground beside him. Taja hesitated only a second before joining him. He set the light against the wall, pointing upwards. "I have to be careful of how much time I spend away from my room. If they ever caught me in here . . . at the very least that would be the end of my explorations."

He leaned his back against the rough rock. "When I was younger I used to imagine being allowed to explore the whole warren. I've heard that these tunnels go right through the mountain to the other side."

"I think they do," Taja said. "And it makes me wonder just how much use Arjun is making of them."

"The reason I asked to meet you is this." He reached into a pocket and pulled out a folded paper. "I tried researching this symbol but I couldn't find anything about it. I was hoping you might recognize it."

Puzzled, she took the paper from him. "It's the Illezie symbol for death, or termination. Ravi--Ravi what is it?" Even in the dim light she could see he'd gone pale. She laid a hand on his shoulder. "Talk to me, Ravi. What's this about?"

He covered her hand with one of his own and shuddered. "Two nights ago, after you got called away, I went to the records room to find out the results of one of my breedings." He shot her a glance as though expecting her to censure him for his curiosity. She merely raised an eyebrow, saying nothing, and he went on to tell her about going through the files and what he'd found.

"Gods and goddesses," Taja whispered, looking at the paper more closely. "That poor woman. All those pregnancies and only two live births."

"She's dead, isn't she?" He looked at her bleakly.

"I . . . I believe so, yes. I'm sorry Ravi." He looked so desolate that she impulsively pulled him into her arms to offer what comfort she could.

"Her usefulness to the Program ended," he whispered. "It happens to us all, in the end."

Taja sat in the semi-dark for a long while, holding Ravi close, her heart breaking for him. She was unable to fool herself any longer. He wasn't just a source of information, or a distraction. He was Kairavini, a beautiful, exciting man, and somehow he had wormed his way into her heart. At last he stirred. She let him go but he stayed close beside her.

"Her name was Ondine," he said. "She was my first, and I was her last. She believed that a breeding was easier if you engaged your emotions instead of suppressing them."

"And was she right?" Taja asked quietly.

"I am not sure. Our last breeding we had no need of the breeding drug, but all my other breedings . . ."

"You and Ondine cared for each other, that made a difference." She had to suppress an unreasonable flash of jealously.

"The men and women in the stories I read . . . they engaged their emotions and needed no drugs to help them. And they engaged in many activities that are not sanctioned in a breeding."

"You mean like kissing?"

"Yes, like kissing. I enjoyed kissing you," he said, voice lowered as though afraid someone else might hear.

Taja laid a palm on his cheek. "I enjoyed kissing you too."

Ravi leaned into her touch, then turned his face and kissed her palm. There was a hitch in her breathing. Taja framed his face with her hands and kissed him gently on the lips. When he started kissing her back she slid her hands downwards, over his shoulders and down his back, pressing closer.

His kisses were soft and gentle at first, but as her mouth opened under his and their tongues began to duel they became harder and more demanding. He took possession of her mouth, there was no other word for it, and it felt oh, so wonderful.

Unable to help herself, she pulled away enough to whisper, "We don't have to stop at kissing."

He pulled back enough to look her in the eyes. "Are you sure about this?"

She took his hands and placed them on the fastenings to her uniform. Slowly he began undoing them; Taja closed her eyes and shivered in anticipation. When he stopped, she opened her eyes in surprise. "What's wrong?"

"Make no mistake," he said, eyes burning with intensity. "I want this. I think I've been waiting all my life for this. But I want our first time together to be special, not fumbling in a dark, cramped, abandoned store room."

"But--"

"You make me feel things I did not know were possible," he whispered against the skin of her neck, nuzzling her just below her ear. His hand caressed her breast through her uniform. "I do not want to breed with you, I want to . . . make love."

"I want that too," she said, sighing as his lips claimed hers again. His kisses left her breathless, his touch left her burning. "Please don't make me wait."

"Tomorrow night," he said, reluctantly pulling away. "I know a place. Meet me at the door after the lights are dimmed. It will be perfect, I promise."

"I'm on duty tomorrow night," she said with a frown.

His groan echoed her own frustration. "The next night then. It will give me time to prepare."

"Prepare? Prepare what? Ravi, I--"

He silenced her with a kiss. "Trust me," he said. "It will be worth the wait. I have a list of things from the stories I want to try."

"What kind of things?" She couldn't stop the shiver of anticipation that went through her.

Ravi grinned. "You'll just have to wait to see."

Kissing her one last time, he reluctantly got to his feet and pulled her up with him. He helped brush the dirt from her uniform, although his touch was more of a caress. Taja was bolder in her assistance, running her hands over his firm ass, then brushing down the front of his trousers as well, eyes widening in appreciation.

"Are you sure you want to wait?" she asked, a mischievous grin on her face.

"Yes," he said, moving her hand away from where it lingered.

Keeping a hold of her hand, he led her back through the tunnels. By the time they reached the security door their breathing was almost back to normal, although they were still slightly flushed. Once back inside the compound properly, they lingered at the door, reluctant to part ways.

"I guess this is it then," she said, unaccountably shy and hating herself for it.

"I look forward to our time together." He kissed her hand and vanished into the dark.

Taja sighed, and wondered just how cold the shower in her quarters could be set to.

Chapter Thirteen

From Nereida's Journal:

There is one way the lives of the M-class greatly differs from those of the Breeders and Seeders, and that is that we are allowed to form and maintain friendships within in our section. As long as we stay behind the heavy, metal security door we are allowed to come and go as we please. Our rooms are small, but we have a common room where we can gather and a small dining hall where we take our meals. The M-section is set far back in the mountain, carved out by the Earth Elementals whose usefulness to the Program had ended. In this, Arjun actually did us a favor. The walls and floors are smoother than a machine could have made them; the roof stronger and safer. He had no choice really, the equipment necessary for such an excavation is forbidden by the colonization charter of this world. But I wonder. Had he the choice, would he have taken such care for our quarters?

With several of the guards still out on the expedition to the outside, it meant the rest of them had to work longer hours. Taja was more than ready for some down time by the time her shift ended. But when she saw the pale blue paper folded into the graceful shape of a bird on the center of her bed, she couldn't help the smile that blossomed on her face, nor the shiver of anticipation that went up her spine.

After a quick shower she dressed in the close fitting, black work out clothes she'd brought with her from Ardraci. Tonight, of all nights, she didn't want Ravi to see her as a guard, but as a woman.

Despite the need for caution, it didn't take her long to make her way to the heavy metal door that separated the compound from the volcano. She was several feet away when she realized there were voices coming from ahead. Staying in the shadows, she moved as close as she dared to listen.

"I'm telling you, there'll be another purging once he's got a new influx of DNA to work with."

It was a man's voice, laced with fear, but Taja was grateful to realize it wasn't Ravi's.

"But that's just amongst the Breeders and Seeders," the woman with him answered. "We've been very careful - he has no reason to get rid of any of the Elementals!"

"Easy for you to say. You're Earth and you're needed in the tunnels. But what do you think's going to happen when he doesn't need you any more?"

There was a moment of silence before the woman answered. "But surely our help counts for something!"

"What do you think happened to our prede-cessors? He's probably already selected our replacements from those ready to be retired from the Program." There was a bitter edge to the man's voice. "Each generation more powerful than the last."

"Is there any way we can escape through the main entrance?" The woman's voice was beginning to sound tearful.

"No. It's too well guarded. If we could only discover where he keeps that map. It may be our only chance . . ."

The voices faded as the couple moved off.

Taja stayed where she was, filing away the information for future use.

"I didn't know there was a map," Ravi said quietly in her ear, his arms coming around her from behind. Somehow, Taja wasn't surprised he'd been watching with her.

"A map would be priceless. You don't think--that couple, they were just . . ."

"I think we need to get out of this corridor." He released her, and tugged her forward by her hand.

With a deft touch, he unlocked the door and they were quickly on the other side.

They were silent as they moved along the passage, although they appeared to be the only ones on the mountain side of the door. Ravi led her down a different tunnel than the one they'd used previously. He moved confidently, as though he'd been this way many times before. When the tunnel they were in branched in two different directions, he stopped.

"Where are we going?" Taja asked.

"You'll find out soon enough," he said, a mischievous grin on his face. "But I want it to be a surprise, so . . ." He pulled a dark blue cloth from his pocket. "Do you trust me?"

"You want to blindfold me?" A shiver went up her spine. "Are you sure it's necessary? It's already almost too dark to see."

"It'll be worth it, I promise."

As he carefully tied the cloth around her head to cover her eyes, Taja found, to her surprise, she did trust him. Perhaps she had been alone for too long, perhaps she was being foolish, but she wouldn't be here with him now if she didn't. She felt the brush of something across her lips, almost too swift and light to be called a kiss, but her lips curved upwards in a smile nonetheless.

They moved slower now. Taja had one hand in Ravi's and the other on the rough wall beside her. She could tell the tunnel they were in was the narrower of

the two. It twisted and turned and as they went past
one particularly sharp bend she stumbled as the rock
under foot turned to sand.

"Sorry," Ravi said, stopping. "I should have
warned you."

"It's fine," Taja told him. "Where are we? Can I
take off the blindfold now?"

"Almost ready. Just stay there for a minute."

It was hard to keep from fidgeting as she heard
him moving around. She felt the heat from his body
as he stood in front of her and all at once his lips
were on hers and then all she could feel was his heat.
Did that small moan come from him or her? It wasn't
until she saw the smug smile on Ravi's face that she
realized he'd taken her blindfold off.

"What? Oh!" Her breath left her in a small gasp as
she stared past him at the chamber they were in.

It was enormous - it seemed to go back forever.
They were on the shore of a subterranean lake, fine
black sand under their feet. It was filled with a soft
glow from the multi-colored, phosphorescent moss
covering the stalactites dripping from the ceiling and a
small light Ravi had set up to reflect back from clear
crystals embedded in the black rock. Several enormous stalagmites were poking up through the placid
water in front of them, ghostly shapes with mirror images.

"Oh, Ravi! This is incredible!"

"This place has always been special to me." He wrapped his arms around her from behind. "Seeing you here, with me . . . now I know why."

"How did you ever find this place?" Taja's voice was hushed. It seemed wrong somehow to speak at a normal volume.

"This is close to where we were trained in the use of our elements. In fact, I'm sure the water in this chamber flows under the rock into the next one. I remember during my training that I sensed a greater source of water than the one we were working with."

"But you don't sense that now?" she asked with a frown.

Ravi shook his head. "No, I'm not powerful enough. When we were training there was a device that enhanced our abilities so we could learn to control them easier."

He released her hand and she followed him over to the blanket he must have spread out earlier that day. He had food and drink there as well. Taja sat down beside him, her frown deepening.

"I read about this in one of the stories." He seemed almost shy. "It's called a picnic."

Mustering up a smile she said, "It's wonderful. I can't remember the last time I was on a picnic, and I've never been on one in such a beautiful place. Ravi," she placed her hand over his, "why do you think your gift isn't powerful?"

"Because it isn't," he said in surprise. "Without the enhancer I would not have passed my training."

Taja chose her next words with care. He needed to know the truth, especially now when forces from outside were closing in. "Ravi . . . what if I told you they lied, that in truth your gift is the most powerful one in, or out, of the Program?"

"Then I'd say you are not familiar with the elemental gifts. Mine was the weakest in the class."

Lacing her fingers through his, she held up his hand. "Why do you wear this band on your wrist?"

"When I came out of my *tespiro* I had powerful headaches. This band keeps them from coming back."

"Did they tell you why you were getting headaches?"

"No, but . . ." It was his turn to frown, remembering. "I remember the technician congratulating me and then telling me I was on my way to becoming a powerful Elemental. But my instructor . . ."

"Your instructor lied," Taja said bluntly. "This," she tapped the cuff, "is an inhibitor. It's designed to suppress your abilities."

* * * * *

Ravi tried to wrap his mind around what she was telling him. It didn't make sense.

Think, brother. Nereida's voice filled his mind. *The device in the cave where you had your lessons . . . it was not to enhance your ability, it was to suppress the inhibitors to allow you a taste of the power that is yours by right.*

But why?

Even though the goal is to breed more powerful Element-als, they fear the very power they create.

How do you know this? And why did you keep this from me?

It would have served no purpose to tell you before. Now . . . now you are ready to hear the truth.

"I don't understand."

"What is the goal of the Program?" Taja asked.

"I . . . to create . . . to . . . I--"

To create the perfect Elemental. Nereida said in his mind. *One that wields all four Elements.*

Letting go of his wrist, Taja laced her fingers through his. "Dr. Arjun believes he can create the perfect Ardraci through controlled breeding. He's starting by creating a group of Elementals who are not only powerful, but pure as well, with no trace of the other elements in them. The next step will be to start cross-breeding until he has an Ardraci who can wield all four elements equally."

"And then what?"

Taja blinked as though the question was not what she expected. "I-I don't know what he intends once he reaches his goal."

He has become so lost in his own Program that I doubt even he knows what his intentions are any more.

This is all so . . . I feel like I should be more shocked, or angry.

Perhaps there is a part of you that senses the upheaval to come, my brother. Time grows short.

I feel so confused.

Put your confusion aside, Kairavini. There is much to be learned tonight, and not all of it will be through talking.

Gentle laughter filled his mind as Nereida's presence vanished.

Ravi looked down to where his hand was joined to Taja's, his thoughts chaotic. There was just one thing he needed to know. "Are you here to stop Dr. Arjun?" he asked bluntly.

Taja hesitated for a long moment but when she spoke, he knew it was the truth. "Yes."

"Good," he said, reaching for her.

Chapter Fourteen

From Nereida's Journal:

There is a long journey ahead of us, and it will begin far too soon. The vision of the volcano grows stronger and each time I have it, I grow weaker. Sta'at lends me what strength she can, but it is never enough. Something to do with her lack of corporeal form . . . or perhaps it is because we share a body and mine is so weak. She still insists I have a purpose, but she is not forthcoming as to what that purpose might be. I begin to wonder what my life would have been like had I been born with a strong enough elemental gift to be useful to the Program. Would it have been better to have a child, only to have that child be taken from me at two years of age so I might have another? Ah, but then I would not have known Sta'at. Nor would Kaine be in my life.

In light of the seriousness of their conversation Taja expected there might have been some distance between them, but a spark flared to life as soon as Ravi touched her. She went willingly into his arms.

Though he held her close, the touch of his lips was tentative, as though he was unsure of his welcome. She began kissing him back but there was something missing. Finally she pulled back so she could see his face.

"Ravi?"

"I don't know what's the matter with me." He shot her a fleeting smile. "I've been with hundreds of women."

"Just what every woman wants to hear," she muttered under her breath.

Ravi didn't realize she'd spoken and continued, "This just feels . . . different somehow."

"Of course it's different," she said softly. She moved around until she was sitting behind him, and stroked her hands over his shoulders, massaging his tense muscles. "Did any of the others touch you like this?"

"Well . . . no." He expelled a breath and she could feel his tense muscles begin to relax.

"How about this," she murmured, kissing the skin of his neck, then taking his earlobe gently between her teeth.

"No," he admitted, with a shiver.

Taja kissed his jaw and then along his throat. "Did any of them ever kiss you like this?"

One hand slid through his hair and guided his head towards her. This kiss was more like the ones she remembered, hard and hungry. His tongue probed at her lips and she opened readily for him. Taja could have kissed him forever, but after a few minutes she pulled back so they could catch their breath.

Somehow she was now in his lap with no memory of how this happened. Not that she was about to complain. "The reason this is different is because this is for you, for us, not for the breeding program. It's the difference between simply breeding and making love."

His eyes were serious as they looked at her. "Is that what we're doing? Making love?"

"Yes," she said, and started kissing him again.

This time she was the aggressor, nipping at his lower lip and easing the sting with a swipe of her tongue. Uncurling her hands from where they were clasped around his neck, she ran them down his chest to the bottom of his tunic. Impatiently she grabbed the hem and began raising it, breaking off their kiss only long enough to pull the tunic over his head. Tossing it aside, she ran her hands over the hard planes of his chest.

Unable to resist, she tweaked his flat, male
nipples. Ravi broke off their kiss with a gasp. "Liked
that did you?" she asked with an impish grin.

"What are you doing?"

He looked faintly alarmed and Taja finally realized
just how lacking in experience he was. "Did none of
the stories you read talk about men and women
touching each other like this?"

"I--I--don't remember."

A slow smile slid across her face. Taking him by
the shoulders, she pushed him flat to the blanket.
"Why don't I teach you about foreplay?"

Ravi didn't know what was wrong with him. He'd
been fantasizing about them being together like this
since reading the first story on the data crystal. It was
all just so much . . . *more* than he'd imagined it to be.

Her hands and her mouth were all over his chest -
licking, biting, sucking. He'd read about the touching
of each other in this way but had no idea it would feel
so . . . exquisite. If he'd been a Fire Elemental they'd
have both gone up in flames. Her hand brushed
against the erection tenting his draw-string pants and
he let out an incoherent cry, hips rising of their own
volition.

Taja lowered herself so that she was lying on top
of him and the feel of the silky material she was wearing, against his bare chest, was almost more than he

could stand. Grabbing her shoulders, he pulled her upwards another few inches so he could start kissing her again. Laughing, she wriggled her way out of his grasp.

"There's more to foreplay than kissing," she told him with a cheeky grin.

"Much more and you just might kill me."

With another laugh she slid herself even further downwards, deliberately rubbing against him. Ravi's groan became a gasp and his hips jerked upwards as she stroked him once through the fabric, then loosened the drawstring of his trousers. When his hips rose she took advantage and pushed the trousers down over his hips, pulling them right off of him.

"Wow," she said.

Ravi's cock twitched in response.

Neither of them were aware of the trembling of the water in the lake beyond.

He was almost afraid to breathe as she stared at him in admiration. Licking her lips, she lowered her head. His shout echoed throughout the cavern as Taja pulled him deep into her mouth.

What was she doing to him? This was definitely not something that would be sanctioned by the breeding program. But oh, the feeling!

Ravi's world narrowed to the sensation of Taja's hot, wet mouth around his cock. Her tongue swirled and caressed him, her hands stroked and squeezed. It was unlike anything he'd ever felt before. She hummed in satisfaction, her cheeks hollowing as she sucked him in deeper, and it was his undoing.

With another cry he jerked upwards, his hot seed spilling into her waiting mouth. She held him firmly, swallowing him down. When he was finished she slowly released him, caressing him with her mouth as she pulled her head away.

"That was--I--I have no words," he said. He was having trouble catching his breath.

Taja rested her head on his thigh. "You taste wonderful," she said.

"I feel as though I have overdosed on the breeding drug."

"That's a terrible analogy," she told him. "The idea here is to make you forget all about the breeding program."

"Perhaps we should try more of this 'foreplay'," he suggested.

Raising her head, Taja smiled up at him. "Perhaps we should."

She moved so she was situated between his legs and then began kissing her way up his torso, mapping his chest with her mouth and hands. His skin where she touched felt like it was on fire, and when she ran her tongue over his nipples the sensation shot straight to his groin. Nothing - not his training, not the stories he'd read - had prepared him for feeling this way.

"Stop!" he gasped.

Taja lifted her head, looking both confused and concerned. "What's wrong? Am I--"

"No, there is nothing wrong," he hastened to re-assure her. "It--I--you . . . you are still fully clothed. I want to touch you was well. Is this 'foreplay' not to be shared?"

"It is indeed."

Gracefully, she slid downwards and then moved over beside him, rising to her knees. Ravi's hand shot out to stop her from undoing the fastening to her tunic. "Wait."

Her brows rose in question.

He levered himself up to a sitting position as well. "Let me."

This was something he would have never dreamed of doing with a Breeder, but then this night was all about stepping beyond his conditioning. He stroked a finger from the base of her throat down to the first fastening of her tunic. Her skin was velvet soft. Taja shivered as slipped his finger underneath the material. There were five fastenings in all, and by the time he'd undone them all they were both breathing heavily.

"Touch me," she demanded, then added, "Please!"

He smiled, and with deliberate slowness pushed the tunic off her shoulders, his hands following it down her arms in a leisurely caress. Impatiently she pulled it the rest of the way off, flinging it to the side.

Ravi swallowed hard and paused as she wriggled out of the rest of her clothing from her seated position.

"I wanted to do that," he protested.

"You were taking too long," she said, unashamedly.

The water in the lake beyond trembled as he gazed in wonder at her naked form. Her breasts were so incredibly soft, and filled his hands perfectly, as though they were meant just for him. He stroked his thumbs over her dark pink nipples and she cried out, arching into his touch.

"I think we need to continue your lesson in foreplay another time. I cannot wait any longer."

Before Ravi realized what she was doing, he was flat on his back again and she was straddling his legs. He was fully aroused once more and there was a smug look on her face. "I think you'll enjoy this even more than foreplay."

"What--" the rest of what he was about to say got lost as his breath left his lungs in a whoosh as she raised up slightly, then lowered again, impaling herself on his rigid cock. They moaned in unison. She was a perfect fit, hot and slick, and when she started to move it was almost more than he could stand.

Ravi thought he'd never seen anything so beautiful as she undulated above him. She was perfect, high firm breasts swaying gently, a slight flush to her pale skin.

They moved together, an exquisite feeling that could never have been found in a mere breeding. Unable to resist, he reached out to stroke her silken flesh, learning the play of muscles under her skin, as she had his. She leaned forward to kiss him, never losing their rhythm and her breasts filled his hands. Taja moaned against his lips as he gently pinched her already taut nipples, making them harden further.

His hips thrust upwards to meet her, trying to push deeper. Neither were aware of the churning lake beyond them. She caught his urgency and began to move faster. Ravi moved his hands to her hips as she straightened up again, a vain attempt to hold her in place as he drove into her. Taja arched her back and they cried out together.

Their movement slowed, then stopped, all but the panting breaths they took. Taja's head hung down and as her breathing eased she slowly collapsed against him. Ravi welcomed her weight, his arms coming around her to hold her close. It was a long time before he was able to speak.

"Next time I wish to taste you, as you did me," he told her.

Taja shivered with anticipation. "I look forward to it."

"Taja, I-I have never . . . I don't . . . I find myself without the words to describe how I am feeling right now."

"Is it a good feeling or a bad feeling?"

He rolled over onto his side and pulled her in for a kiss. "It is most definitely a good feeling. A very happy feeling."

She smiled and ran the back of her hand over his cheek. "That's the way it's supposed to be."

"Every time?"

She couldn't hold back a laugh at his surprise. "Yes, every time."

"I don't want to go back. I want to stay here, with you," Ravi said as they lay entwined on the blanket, resting.

"We have some time left."

He let out a gusty sigh. "You don't understand. I don't want to go back . . . ever."

"Oh, Ravi." She leaned over and gave him a lingering kiss. "It won't be for much longer, I promise."

Her stomach chose that moment to give a loud gurgle. Taja blushed as Ravi sat up properly, pulling her up beside him.

"You're hungry," he said. "You must allow me to feed you."

"I must?"

"Yes," he said firmly, reaching for the bottle of wine he'd pilfered from one of the store rooms. "There was a story in which the participants fed each other. It lead to some quite interesting times."

"Did it now?" Taja asked with a slow smile. Her mouth opened to comment further but she was distracted by the sight just over his shoulder. "Ravi, look."

Curious, he turned. "What am I looking at?"

"The lake, the water . . ."

The water was moving, as though settling down from a larger disturbance. The black sand along its edge was wet, as were the rocks closest to it.

"I don't understand. Was there a seismic disturbance we were unaware of?"

"I think there is a simpler explanation than that." Taja reached for his hand. "Often my sister, when she is with her *enjulla*, loses control of her element."

"You believe I am responsible for the movement of the water? That I was able to call forth my element?" The full meaning of what she said sunk in. "Wait, your sister is an Elemental?"

Taja nodded her head, eyes on his face. "She is a very powerful Wind Elemental."

"But you . . ."

"I do not have an elemental gift."

"How is this possible?"

His bewilderment seemed to reassure her.

"All of you in the Program, including Dr. Arjun, come from a world called Ardraci."

"Ardraci," he repeated. "How did we get here?"

"Dr. Arjun and his followers left Ardraci in ships. I have no idea why he chose this planet, but he settled here to continue his experiments many years ago. We've been looking for him for a very long time."

"All right, but how is it that your sister is an Elemental, yet you are not?"

"All Elementals are Ardraci, but not all Ardraci are Elementals. When we reach the age of *tespiro* we are given the choice of learning to control our gift, or having our gift blocked. My sister showed signs of her power even before *tespiro* while I . . . did not. My gift was minor, and though it still would have required training it would never have amounted to much. I did not wish to spend my life being compared to my sister and so I chose to have my gift suppressed."

Ravi just stared at her, a shocked expression on his face. "Say something," Taja said.

In a world where power was everything, what she just told him bordered on blasphemy. Willingly suppressing an elemental gift? How would one know their place in the Program?

"It's all right," she said, reaching for her clothes. "I understand if you no longer wish to be with me."

That snapped Ravi out of wherever his mind had gone. "What? No!" He reached for her, pulling her into his arms. "Why would you think that?"

She sagged against him. "I feared you would see me differently, knowing I gave up my gift," she said, voice muffled against his neck.

"Taja, I did not know of your gift when we first met, and still I was attracted to you." He pulled away slightly to look at her. "Why are you smiling?"

"I like the way my name sounds when you say it."

"And I liked the way you called out my name just a short while ago," he said with a grin.

He lowered his head slightly and kissed her. Taja sighed and began kissing him back. Her stomach chose that moment to gurgle again. Ravi pulled away with a laugh.

"I'm sorry," she said, a faint flush of embarrassment on her face.

"I did say I would feed you," he reminded her, reaching for the basket of food. "You can tell me about this planet you say we are from while we eat. What was it called again?"

"Ardraci," she told him.

* * * * *

"What were you looking for the night we met in the records room?" he asked as they rested, staring out at the underground lake. Ravi's back was propped up against one of the rocks and Taja cuddled into his side.

Taja sighed. "Something, anything, that would give me a clue as to how to bring Arjun down with minimal casualties."

A frontal assault would be useless, he'd just move everyone deeper into the cave system.

Ravi repeated Nereida's words out loud, wondering how long Nereida had been eavesdropping.

Her laughter filled his mind. *Do not fear, my brother. I am not quite the voyeur you think I am.*

"His filing system is a nightmare," Taja was saying, and with a start he realized he'd missed the first part of what she said. "He's got this wonderful classification system, but there still seems to be no discernible key to the filing of these records."

"Do you know what the different classifications are?" he asked, tensing up.

Ravi, no!

"Well, yes, of course. Why do--"

"What is the M class?" he asked, cutting off what she was going to say. He felt a wave of unhappiness from Nereida, but ignored it.

"Oh, the M class." She gave a little shiver. "If we can save only one group from this place, I hope it's them."

"Why?" He sat up so he could look at her properly. She looked sad, but he had to know.

"They're the ones whose gifts were too weak to be of any use to the breeding program."

"What happens to them?"

Ravi, please don't.

"Well, the lucky ones become technicians."

"And the unlucky ones?" he asked quietly.

"Why do you want to know?" Taja sat up as well and placed a hand on his arm. "Ravi, what is it?"

"Tell me the rest."

She sighed. "The unlucky ones are given to the guards as . . . a kind of stress relief, I guess you could call it. Ravi? What's wrong?"

Ravi could feel a great rage building inside him. The water in the lake began to tremble. "Nereida, why didn't you tell me?" He didn't even realize he'd spoken out loud.

It was not something to share with a brother, Nereida said unhappily. *And there was nothing you could have done.*

"Who's Nereida?" Taja asked at the same time.

"I would have found some way to stop it," Ravi vowed. "All these years . . . How could I not have known?"

I was careful and guarded my thoughts and emotions. I had hoped you would never find out.

"Ravi, who are you talking to?"

He turned to Taja and opened his mouth, but nothing came out.

Tell her.

"Nereida is my twin sister."

Chapter Fifteen

From Nereida's Journal:

One of the ways my visions differ than others who have them, and Sta'at assures me that it is more common than I would believe, is that I sometimes see into the past, as well as the future. Most of the time when this happens I see people or things that have no meaning to me, but the ones Sta'at finds most interesting are the visions I have of Uri Arjun. I have seen his childhood, and how his mother blamed the Illezie for his father's death. I have seen the way he shunned all comfort when his mother was taken from him, arrested for crimes against the Illezie and sent to a penal colony. And I know the reason behind his steadfast rule regarding anyone forming an attachment. Years ago Dr. Arjun himself fell in love with one of his Breeders. She was a Fire Elemental, like him, and died giving birth to their child. He believes the child died as well, but I saw that he was the first of those who were rescued from the compound. It was after that that Arjun became truly paranoid, seeing plots conspiracies everywhere, culling those he thought could not be trusted from his staff. Were it not for the fact that I am one of those who are paying the price for his madness, I could almost feel sorry for him.

Taja's eyes were wide as she repeated the word. "Sister?"

Ravi looked at her warily. "I'm sorry I didn't tell you before, but--"

"Growing up in this place, I think I understand," she said. "You have a sister, a twin sister. And you can talk to each other mind to mind?" Her eyes searched his for confirmation. "But . . . how is this possible?"

"I don't know how we are able to talk mind to mind," he said. "I've always thought it was some sort of genetic mutation --"

"No," Taja said, reaching for their clothes. "I meant how is it possible that you have a twin. I would have thought Arjun wouldn't allow it."

"I don't know how our mother managed to carry us to term without Arjun knowing." He took the clothes Taja handed him and began pulling them on, filled with regret that their time together was ending this way. "I suspect she had help."

She did, Nereida confirmed. *It was a midwife named Wynne.*

"What? How do you know?"

Wynne was my friend - she knew things . . .

"What do you mean she knew things? The same way you knew things?"

"Who knew things?" Taja asked. "Your sister?

Tell her everything, Nereida said.

Ravi ran a hand through his hair. "Nereida knows things, it's true, but she tells me there was a midwife who helped our mother."

"There was a small group of staff members who secretly worked against Arjun," Taja said slowly. "She must have been one of them."

They died when we moved from the old compound to this one.

Ravi relayed what his sister said.

"When we were taken from our mother we were separated -"

"How old were you?"

"Two. We were sent to separate nurseries . . ."

Where it was believed we would forget about each other, Nereida put in.

Ravi repeated what she said, and added, "But when we didn't we were told we were no longer brother and sister and were not to acknowledge each other in that way."

So we learned to pretend.

"Yes, for years we pretended we meant nothing to each other, living in fear that they would truly separate us if we showed any kind of feeling towards each other."

"Oh, Kairavini." There was a world of heartbreak in her voice and she reached out to touch the back of his hand.

And in the end we were separated, Nereida said sadly. *Just as everyone is kept separate in this place.*

"Arjun needs to pay for this. *I* will make him pay. Bad enough he would have let you die during our *tespiro*, but this . . ."

On this we agree, my brother. Arjun must be made to pay for his crimes.

"Ravi, you need to calm yourself."

He was brought out of his reveries at Taja's urgent tone, her hand clutching his arm. "What . . ." His voice trailed off as he looked at the lake.

The water was churning as though there was a tide rushing in.

"What's happening?" he whispered.

It's you, my brother. You are the one affecting the water.

"You need to calm down," Taja said at the same time. "Your element is being impacted by your strong emotions."

"That's not possible." Ravi shook his head in denial. "My gift--"

"Your gift is so powerful that even with the inhibitor you wear your element is affected when you experience strong emotions, like anger."

Or love, Nereida added.

Ravi stared at the churning water.

You don't know what you're talking about, he told Nereida.

You cannot hide your feelings from me, she told him. *Who knows you better than I?*

The water began to calm. *What am I to do?*

For now you need to return to your rooms. Things will be moving very quickly, very soon.

"Nereida says it's time we return," he said reluctantly.

Taja's eyes searched his, but she merely nodded and finished dressing. Ravi had the feeling she was expecting him to say something else, but he had no idea what it could be. Nereida was silent, as though she expected something as well but thought he should work it out himself.

Things seemed a little awkward between them as he led the way back down the tunnels, but he couldn't pin point what had changed. He wracked his brain, trying to remember how such things went in the stories he'd read.

"You mentioned your sister can see things," Taja said, breaking the silence between them. "Can she see what happens in the future?"

"Sometimes," Ravi said. "I suspect she sees more than she shares with me."

I share always that which you need to know. And now, brother, I believe you need to share.

Share what?

There was a heartfelt, disembodied sigh. *Your feelings. Unless you wish Taja to believe what you shared meant little more to you than any breeding.*

But she knows - I already told her --

How can you not realize she is as uncertain as you? Do you think this is something she does often?

Well . . .

Kairavini!

They had reached the main tunnel where it was wide enough to walk side by side. Ravi slanted a glance towards Taja.

She is very much like the women in the stories I read . . . I do not believe what we shared holds the significance for her that it does for me.

How can I have such an idiot for a brother? Nereida's wave of annoyance hit him in the head like a slap.

Ravi stumbled in the dark tunnel. Nerieda projected an angry burst of words that he could make little sense of. Something about sharing feelings and all men being imbeciles and women not being mind readers.

He glanced at Taja again. The stories that he'd read . . . they'd often ended with the two in question forming a permanent attachment. Would such a thing be possible with Taja? It would not be possible in the compound, but if they were free . . .

Ravi stopped in front of the metal security door, suddenly understanding what Nereida was trying to tell him.

"I need to say something."

Taja looked at him, brows lifted in question.

"We have only had stolen moments to be with each other. This, what we shared . . . " He sighed heavily. "It is difficult for me to speak of feelings that I have been told all my life I must not have."

Taja reached up, cupping his cheek. "I understand."

He turned his head so he could kiss her palm. "I want more than just stolen moments."

"I want that too," she whispered.

"Before we return I need you to know. I . . . care about you. I care deeply, with the depth of feeling I have for my sister, but I do not feel in any way as a brother should towards you. What I feel is . . . so much more."

"Oh, Ravi." Tears pricked at her eyes and she kissed him, then held him close. "I love you too," she whispered in his ear.

His arms tightened around her. "You have ruined me," he said, stroking his hands up and down her back. "I can no longer fulfill my duty as a Seeder. No--" he said as she would have protested. "This is a good thing. How could I take part in something so cold, now that I have known your warmth?"

Do not fear, my brother. There will be no more breedings. Many things will be changing in a very short span of time. I pray you are both ready for it.

* * * * *

You are late with your report.

"It couldn't be helped," Taja said, grateful she was speaking using the E.T.T. with the Illezie instead of a com-link. It would only take one look for an Illezie to know what she'd been up to.

Well?

"Sorry. The breedings are still suspended, but there's been a great deal of activity in the labs. I haven't been able to get close enough for confirmation, but I have reason to believe equipment is being moved."

At least that's what the note from Kairavini said. This one had been folded in the shape of a fish, waiting for her on her bed when she got back from her extended shift. It also said it was getting harder to move around without being seen but there was an abandoned passage near the big security door where they could meet. He even drew her a map.

He has been using low atmosphere transport ships in stealth mode to move equipment to an as yet unknown location.

"You think he's going to move the whole compound? No . . ." For some reason she suddenly remembered Ravi telling her about seeing people taken under guard into the tunnels and the guards returning alone. "He's only moving select parts of it. But why would he leave the rest behind?"

There has been an increase in seismic activity. It is our belief that once he has those he finds useful installed in his new lab, he will trigger an eruption that will deal with those he leaves behind.

"By the gods," Taja whispered. "But how . . ."

She was about to question Arjun's ability to keep everyone he wished to dispose of in the complex, but remembered the mag lock on the door leading to the tunnel system, and the one just like it on the door to the outside. There were also locks on the doors to each section and all the rooms within them. She went over to her own door and realized for the first time it had a lock that could be overridden by a remote source.

"He's going to lock in everyone he's not taking with him and leave us to die in the eruption."

Indeed.

Taja's first impulse was to tell her fellow guards what was going on in hopes that they could be persuaded into helping get the innocent to safety when the time came. But these guards were paid well to follow orders without question. They were an incurious lot, hand picked to be that way. They were also hardened mercenaries who would care nothing for the people left behind.

There has been an altercation in the city. It will not be long before the children from the village will arrive and will be temporarily housed near the main doors. They must be your priority.

"Why them? Why not those who have suffered the most under Arjun's madness?"

When the time comes, we will have a team waiting for them on the outside.

Somehow, she wasn't surprised when her question was ignored. "And the others?"

Save as many as you can. Save yourself. Find help where you can.

With that the Illezie's presence in her mind vanished.

Taja shivered. Normally she would find the meditation pose she adopted to talk mind to mind relaxing, but this time she was too tense to relax. The task before her was daunting. She was just one person, how was she to save all these innocents?

You are not alone.

The voice had a distinctive feminine ring to it. Taja sat up straight. "Dah'mat?" Who else could it be but her Illezie friend? But the voice was gone again.

It was true though, she wasn't really alone. She could count on Ravi to help her, and probably his sister as well. Who knew how many others there were, they just had to find them.

True to her contact's word, the special team arrived the next day, followed a few days later by a second team who'd been involved in the disturbance in the city. This team brought in a single young woman, and appeared to have paid dearly for the effort.

Try as she might, Taja could find no way of getting close to her to both reassure her that she wasn't alone and to ensure her co-operation when it came time to move. Being familiar and the oldest, the children would listen to her where they might not to a stranger.

She couldn't get close to her, but maybe there was someone else who could . . .

Chapter Sixteen

From Nereida's Journal:

I *have had another vision. This one is even more terrifying than the volcano erupting. There is a world in turmoil, light years away from here. Light years away from anywhere in known space, yet at the center of everything. The seas are poisonous and hold fantastic creatures; the atmosphere full of gaseous clouds of untold colors swirling together. The inhabitants of the land masses are unlike any creature I have ever seen. On an island in the sea lays a temple-like structure and within the temple lays a square surrounding a circle, alien symbols carved into the stone between the two. Though I do not know the language, I know the symbols represented the four elements. The image in my mind seemed to shiver, and then five cloaked figures entered the temple, one for each of the four corners of the square and one in the center. I believe they were human, though I could not see past the hoods of their cloaks. A sonorous voice proclaimed: "Behold, the Five Who Are the One." I could feel Sta'at listening in as I related this vision to Kaine; though she shares my mind she does not share what I see. He has become quite adept at helping me interpret what is to come. But it was not the fact that Kaine had never heard of such a world that frightened me so, it was feeling Sta'at's complete and utter shock at what I described.*

"Are you sure about this?" Dr. Arjun demanded, reading the report once again.

"Yes, sir. I saw him myself. We were totally unprepared for two of them; I deeply regret we were unable to secure him as well."

"It is unfortunate, yes . . . You say he was protecting the girl?"

"That's right sir. They appeared to be a couple."

Dr. Arjun frowned. "That helps to explain why she is being so difficult now. But Fire and Water . . . she had best get that thought out of her head as quickly as possible."

Cullen, the security chief, remained silent.

"And you say they had taken refuge in the Temple of Nishon."

"Yes sir.

"Damn priests. There's rumors they have ties to the Illezie." Arjun's fingers drummed against the desk top. "It's just as well we've already begun preparing for our move. Looks like we need to move up our time table."

"Yes sir!"

* * * * *

Ravi lay hidden in the air vent for close to an hour before he determined it was safe enough to approach the door he was watching. This section of the compound had been unused, off limits, until recently when the guards that had been sent out returned with a group of strangers. Now it was the busiest section of the compound.

Despite their isolation, information still found its way to the members of the Program. It was rumored these strangers were part of the Program who had been living elsewhere. Ravi didn't see how this was possible, but Taja confirmed it.

He'd been unable to refuse when she asked if he could check on the last outsider to arrive. The others had been brought in as a group; this last one had arrived alone under heavy guard. Taja wanted to make contact herself, but it would be far too dangerous for her to be caught in this section.

"Take some time to think about it," she said. "If you're caught . . ."

You must do this, my brother. Nereida's voice whispered through his mind.

What? Why?

The newcomer . . . she is the one from my vision. She is . . . she will be important. She --

"Forget I asked," Taja said, misunderstanding the reason for his silence. "It's too risky, even for you."

He shrugged, flashing her a grin. "If I'm caught I'll just put it down to curiosity about the newcomers."

W*ho is she?* he sent out. *Why is she so important? Nereida?*

But Nereida had vanished again and now here he was. With quiet proficiency he removed the grill from the vent and slithered through the opening, replacing it once he was in the corridor. He was lucky, the vent was almost directly across from the door he sought.

He hesitated outside the door. Should he knock? The sound of approaching footsteps warned him that he only had a few seconds before the security guard patrolling this corridor would be here. It came as no surprise the door was locked; it only took a second for him to get past the lock and before the guard rounded the corner the door was clicking shut behind him.

The room was surprising. It was not stark, like he was used to. The furnishings were mostly wood, not plastic and metal. There was paper on the walls with a bright floral print on it. Part of one wall was hidden behind hanging yellow fabric and there was more fabric on the floor.

The girl was curled up on her bed, but he didn't think she was sleeping. When he touched her lightly on the arm she flinched and rolled away from him.

"I'm sorry," he said quietly. "I didn't mean to startle you. I just . . . are you all right?"

"All right? All right?" Her voice rose in volume as she uncurled herself and sat up. "I've been kidnapped and held against my will, I've been poked and prodded within an inch of my life, and some lunatic has told me I'm going to be used in some kind of breeding program. What makes you think I'd be all right?" She stared so hard at him he backed away a few steps. "Who are you?"

Ravi's voice caught in his throat. She looked very familiar, and not just because she was obviously a Water Elemental. It was like he knew her, like he'd been the one having visions of her instead of Nereida. She looked very similar to Nereida - same slight build, blonde hair and blue eyes, maybe a couple of years younger.

"You're gifted like me, aren't you?" she asked. "Your gift is Water."

Ravi pulled himself together and tried to smile reassuringly at her, but kept his distance. "That's right, I'm a third generation Water Elemental. My name is Kairavini, but you can call me Ravi if you like. What's your name?"

"I'm Rayne," she said after a moment's hesitation. Then she frowned. "Third generation, what do you mean?"

"Just what it sounds like. My parents, and their parents before them, were all Water Elementals."

"You're part of this breeding program, aren't you?" she whispered. She moved to the other side of the bed, putting it between them. "Is that why you're here? I'm warning you right now, I have no intention of creating a fourth generation with you."

"Relax, that's not why I'm here. I just thought—" Ravi sighed and ran a hand through his hair. This was not going the way he'd intended. This first visit was supposed to be about reassuring her, winning her trust. "I'm not supposed to be here. I just thought you might be needing a friend."

"A friend?" she repeated, voice laced with suspicion. "Is that what you are?"

"I could be. At the very least I can try and answer some of your questions. Look, do you mind if I sit down?" He hoped she'd find him less of a threat if he was sitting down.

She shrugged, and he took that as permission to make himself comfortable in one of the chairs. Nereida had been so adamant that he be here he fully expected her to be watching through his eyes, but when he reached out to her with his mind he found the way blocked. Rayne continued to watch him warily.

"All right, friend, you say you can answer my questions so answer me this, how do I get out of here?"

Ravi shook his head. "I don't know." When she opened her mouth to protest he held up his hands. "Honestly, I don't. I've never been to the outside. There's never been any reason to."

"You've never been outside of this place?" She sounded horrified by the idea. "You've never seen the grass or the trees, never seen the sky at night, filled with stars?"

"I was born and raised in the compound," he told her, and except for that one terrifying night when he was a child and they moved from the old compound to this one, he'd never even seen a window to the outside. "Some day, when my usefulness is over, I'll die here."

At least that's what he'd always believed. Before he would not have questioned his place, but being with Taja changed him more than he realized. Was it possible he was actually starting to believe they could escape this place?

"How can you be so offhand about it?"

He tried to be reassuring, but was he reassuring her or himself? "I can't miss what I've never had. This is all I've ever known."

She stared at him and he tried not to fidget. It was on the tip of his tongue to tell her about the plans to free them, but he held off. Unless Taja and her friends were successful, this was going to be her life now and she might as well start getting used to it. He felt a wave of pity for her, and with a rare flash of empathy knew she was feeling the same for him.

"How many others with the Water gift are there?"

Ravi shrugged. "In my year group there's nine. But only three others are pure Water."

"What do you mean, pure water?"

"I mean their parents were both water as well. There are only a few pure Elementals left. Of course there are many others that have been crossed with Water."

"What about your parents?"

"What about them?" he asked in surprise. No one ever speculated about their parentage. It was enough to know they were both pure Water.

"How can they let this happen?"

She seemed genuinely distressed about it, just as Taja had been. Ravi couldn't fathom why. "I don't understand. It's what we're here for."

"But don't you talk to them about it?"

"There's no one to talk to," he told her. "Men are kept in a different section of the compound. Children are kept with their mothers for the first two years, then transferred to the nursery until they reach *tespiro*. If they survive, they're given their own rooms."

"That's horrible!"

Ravi had assumed these newcomers had come from another compound, they had to have been products of the Program otherwise they wouldn't be fit as breeding stock, but he was beginning to realize that they must have truly grown up in the outside. Is this why Nereida believed Rayne was so important to them? Because she could tell them first hand what it was like outside?

"What about siblings? How do you know if someone else is a brother or sister or just a friend?"

"Breeding is strictly controlled. Cross-breeding between siblings would result in genetic degradation. As for friends . . . we aren't really encouraged to socialize – it's too tempting to form attachments and that's strictly forbidden."

"Why?"

"It makes it too hard if you get attached to the wrong person," he said quietly.

"I don't understand."

He sighed and scraped his hand through his hair. "Say you make friends with someone and he cares deeply for a woman. But when it comes time for her to be bred you're chosen instead of him. What would that do to your friendship? And worse, what if she had an attachment for him as well?" He shook his head. "No, it would just make things so much worse."

"But surely if the two they wish to b-b-breed do not care for each other . . ." Rayne swallowed hard. "There are artificial means to do so."

"Feelings don't enter into it," he told her gently. At least they weren't supposed to. "And Dr. Arjun believes he gets better results with the old fashioned method."

"But . . . What if you refuse? Surely they can't force . . ."

Ravi shivered slightly and looked at her bleakly. "Trust me, they can." That's what the breeding drugs were for. He'd only had to take part in one Breeding where his partner had to be restrained - it still haunted him. Even heavily dosed as she was there were still tears in her eyes as she pleaded with him not to do it. He had to request extra drugs for both of them to get through it.

"If socializing is discouraged," Rayne said finally, "How were you able to come here?"

Ravi was grateful for the change in topic. "They're a little short on guards right now, and Arjun's in an unusually good mood. One of the newcomers brought in is a potential Fire Elemental."

Rayne straightened up. "That's my sister! What have they done to her?"

Ravi mentally cursed. So much for putting her at her ease. It was on the tip of his tongue to ask how she ended up with a fire gifted sister, but one look at her face and he hastened to reassure her instead.

"Relax, she's fine! Fire Elementals are rare; they won't let anything happen to her. They'll take very good care of her."

"And then they'll breed her, like she's some kind of animal," she said bitterly.

"Not right away, she hasn't been through her *tespiro* yet."

"How soon?"

"How soon after her *tespiro*? A year, maybe more. It depends on whether or not he finds a suitable . . .

partner." He stopped suddenly as the obvious choice occurred to him.

"What? What is it?"

"It's nothing," he mumbled, unable to look at her.

"Tell me!"

"It's just . . . Dr. Arjun. I've heard that his element is fire."

Rayne stared at him, the blood leaving her face. "My sister, and th-th-that old man? But that's—no! I won't let that happen!"

There was genuine pity in his eyes as he looked at her. "There won't be anything you can do to stop it if that's what he decides."

She continued to stare at him, tears filling her eyes. Ravi wished he could say something, anything, to make her feel better. He wished he could start this whole visit over again.

"I'm sorry. It wasn't my intention to upset you. I'm sure Arjun's too old to make a viable candidate. There are so few pure Fires left that he's not going to take any chances with --" He stopped before he made things even worse. "I should probably leave before I'm missed." He rose to his feet and went to the door where he stopped to look back at her. "I shouldn't have come here. I'm sorry."

"Why did you come?"

Because a woman he was forbidden to care for asked him to, and the sister he wasn't supposed to know he had insisted on it. "I overheard some of the technicians talking about the new subjects that were brought in and the hard time they were having adjusting to the compound." That part was true enough, and it was no wonder they were having a hard time adjusting if they were raised on the outside. "I thought . . . I just thought I could help put you at your ease. I think I've only made things worse for you and for that I truly am sorry."

He stood for a moment as though waiting for her to speak and when she didn't he slipped through the door. The lock clicked into place behind him.

* * * * *

Back in his own room, Ravi threw himself on his bed.

She is stronger than you give her credit for, Nereida's voice whispered through his mind. *And she needed to know the truth about what lies ahead.*

Maybe so, but you didn't see the look on her face.

Oh, my brother, her voice sighed through his mind. *It will not be long before her anguish turns to anger, and that anger will sustain her through what is to come.*

You know what's to come, don't you? Ravi sat up on the bed. *Care to share?*

Little has changed from what I told you before. Although . . . I know that you and Taja play a role in saving many from the flames, including the outsiders. And I have seen the bond between you and Taja and it gladdens my heart.

A *bond? What kind of bond?* He didn't know why the idea appealed to him so much. Seeders didn't form bonds . . . of any kind.

I*t is a bond that will sustain you, just as Rayne's anger will sustain her. I see you and your guardswoman near a great body of water. She--it is in the not so distant future.*

Y*our visions are becoming more frequent - this worries me greatly, sister.*

Y*ou always worry about me, brother.* Nereida laughed in his mind.

D*on't try to change the subject. When we were younger you only had your visions occasionally, but they took a lot out of you when you did. How are you able to manage now that you're having them so frequently?*

Nereida was silent for so long that he thought she'd left. *Kairavini*, she said at last. *Do not fear for me. I promise you this, the visions will not trouble me for much longer.*

Far from being comforted, Ravi felt a chill at her words.

Chapter Seventeen

From Nereida's Journal:

My *thoughts are becoming erratic, I am having trouble focusing
on the present. My mind is too filled with the future. The visions of the volcano grow strong enough that I can feel its heat,
smell the sulfur in the air. And there have been a series of mild
tremors that no one is able to ignore. Yet still we are told all is
well, there is nothing to fear. Other than Kaine, few visit us
now, and never for long.*

The *vision of the temple incapacitated me for a number of days.
Kaine wanted to take me to the infirmary but my friends insisted he not. It is not wise to draw attention to yourself when
you are an M-class, and how would he explain what was
wrong with me? Tell them I was having problems recovering
from the intensity of the vision I'd had? He would have earned
a quick death for himself for discovering such a thing, and as*

for me . . . they would have dissected my brain to see how such an anomaly was possible so they could either exploit it, or prevent it from happening again.

Taja was getting better at sensing when Ravi was near. This time she wasn't startled at all when his arms came around her from behind.

"I've missed you," he said, nuzzling her neck.

"I've missed you too," she admitted. She started to relax in his arms but all at once stiffened with resolve. "Stop that," she said, wriggling free.

"But--"

She put her fingers over his lips. "I need your help again."

He made a face. "Are you sure? You saw where my help got you with Rayne."

"When things start happening they will go very quickly. We need to be prepared."

"I was already prepared," he muttered. "How can I help?"

"I need you to talk to your sister, and anyone else you think might help us when the time comes. Most importantly, we need to find a map of the cave system. I think Arjun plans on taking people out that way - we need to be able to follow him."

"There are one or two from my childhood who might be persuaded to help," Ravi said, though there was too much doubt in his voice for her liking. "I will visit them later."

"No, you need to do this as soon as possible."

"Are you sure about that?" He reached for her again. "I've been reading the data cube again and--"

"Ravi!" She twisted out of his reach. He was altogether too tempting "There will be plenty of time later. You can do whatever you want once we're free."

"I want to be with you forever."

"Don't say that." She said it without thinking and immediately wished she could take the words back.

Ravi pulled back, a hurt look on his face. "You do not wish to be with me once we are free of this place?"

"No, that's not what I meant at all," Taja was quick to reassure him. "But you might change your mind once you've gotten used to freedom and all the things it has to offer."

"Never." He pulled her close again and rested his cheek against her head. "Freedom would mean nothing without you to share it with."

She returned his embrace, his words meaning more to her than she could possibly say.

* * * * *

Once again they met in one of the dead end tunnels that riddled the inner part of the compound.

"How did it go?"

Ravi sighed. "It went as I expected. I spoke only to those I could trust . . . Some are missing, most do not believe there is any threat to their lives, despite the tremors we've been experiencing, nor do they give credit to rumors regarding the compound being moved. Many will not involve themselves in anything that may seem contrary to Dr. Arjun's wishes."

"But don't they wish to be free?"

"You must understand, Taja, we have lived all our lives within the compound. The outside is just as frightening as staying here is. For some it is even more frightening."

"I had hoped . . . never mind." She shook her head. "I forget that for all intents and purposes you've all been conditioned to this life. It breaks my heart."

He moved closer to her. "And me? Do I break your heart?"

She reached up and cupped the side of his face. "You could quite easily break my heart most of all," she whispered.

Leaning closer he kissed her gently, and when she didn't pull away he deepened it. For a moment she kissed him back before pulling back. She did not, however, pull completely away, taking what comfort she could while she could.

"I was just a child when the compound was moved, but I still remember that day," he told her in a quiet voice. He folded his arms around her and held her close. "It was terrifying. We were loaded into transports and flown to this location in the dead of night. The building wasn't finished yet and we had to camp out doors. I remember a lot of screaming and crying, but I also remember touching a tree in the dark – the roughness of its bark, the stickiness of the sap, the smell of it . . ."

"Oh, Ravi."

"I remember hoping at the time we'd be outside long enough to see the sun, but we were inside again before sunrise." He looked down at her. "I think freedom is something I will enjoy getting used to."

"Freedom is not something you should have to get used to," Taja said fiercely. "It is something you should be born to."

"I'm beginning to understand, thanks to you."

She smiled tremulously. "Good. I just wish we had time to make the others understand as well."

"I tried, but . . ." he shrugged helplessly. "There is something else. One of the Breeders has noticed that the children are missing, along with many of the medical and research staff."

Taja nodded. "It looks like Arjun has already started moving the ones he's taking with him to the new location. Could you tell if anyone else is missing?"

"No, but the doors of the personal quarters have been marked, either a red or green symbol on them - including mine."

"Let me guess, yours is a green symbol?"

He nodded. "Yes, as is anyone with a rating of four or higher."

Taja swore under her breath.

"There is a small number of those who will help. And others may join us once they realize the danger is real."

Maybe, but Taja had her doubts. These people were like animals who'd been in their cages too long. No matter how dangerous it became, they felt safer in those cages.

"At least that's something." For Ravi's sake she tried to stay positive. "Let's just hope it's not too late."

"What happens now?"

"Now, we get ready." Taja was all business again. She pulled a hand-drawn map of the compound from her back pocket and unfolded it. "Here's where the outsiders are quartered. We need to get them to this point here before all hell breaks loose."

"All hell?"

"Yes. I have friends on the outside who will be arranging a distraction and then they'll be breaking through the gates. At that point the priority is to get as many of the children out as possible."

"When do we start?"

"We're just wait—" she stopped, head held to one side as though listening. "We start now."

"Now? How do you know?"

She started to lead the way out of the tunnel. "I was fitted with an E.T.T., an Esper Thought Transfer device. It allows limited thought communication. I was just told that we need to get ready."

"But the guards . . ." he almost had to jog to keep up with her.

"The guards will have better things to worry about than what we're doing, trust me."

"I do trust you," he said soberly. "I wouldn't be doing this otherwise."

Taja stopped suddenly. "I know I'm asking a lot of you," she began.

He placed his fingers to her lips. "You're asking nothing of me I'm not willing to give."

* * * * *

"Report!" Dr. Arjun snapped.

"There's a small group up on the ridge outside the security barrier. We've detected a ship in orbit and can only assume there'll be reinforcements," Cullen told him.

"Damn it! We're not ready. Sacrifices will have to be made." Arjun paced from one side of the room to the other. "The staff and children are already in place, but we'll need to start moving the others immediately. You have your priority list?"

"Yes, sir." Cullen hesitated, and then, "Forgive me sir, but why don't we use the transport ships to move the personnel as well? It would be faster, and less risky."

Arjun was already shaking his head. "The risk of being discovered if the ships are scanned far outweighs any risk of traversing the tunnels. We are disappearing, Cullen. And if it is believed we perished in the mountain -- so much the better."

"Yes, sir," Cullen said. If he had any other thoughts about the insanity of moving such a large group of people through the tunnel system of the mountain, he wisely kept them to himself.

"Remember, the Water and Wind Elementals in front to clear the way, and the Fire and Earth Elementals bring up the rear to collapse the tunnels behind us."

"Yes, sir. What about the others?"

"We stick with the plan. They've served their purpose. We'll put them on lockdown when we leave. Let the volcano take care of them."

* * * * *

Taja found Kairavini a guard's uniform, and though he felt somewhat foolish wearing it, he could see the sense of it. Together they ran back to the main part of the compound.

"The outsider children are close to the main entrance. I'll get them to the outside while you get Rayne," Taja told him.

"What about the others?"

"We'll come back for them."

A warning klaxon sounded just as they reached the main corridor of the compound.

"Is that smoke?" Ravi asked.

Taja nodded. "It's part of the distraction I mentioned. Don't worry, it's under the control of a Fire Elemental. Now go, we don't have a lot of time."

Ravi grabbed her arm as she turned towards the passageway that would lead her to the children and swung her around into his arms, kissing her fiercely.

"Stay safe," he told her. "We'll met at the main entrance."

"May luck be with us both," she said. She kissed him back and he let her go.

Ravi relayed what was happening to Nereida. *You need to get out of your room now. Meet us at the main entrance.*

I *will, my brother.*

He reached the room where Rayne was being kept and made short work of the lock.

"Ravi!" she exclaimed. "What are you doing here? What is that noise? What's going on?" With each question her voice rose a little higher.

"You have friends who have come to rescue you," he told her. "We don't have much time, we have to hurry."

"Pyre!"

The way her face lit up, Ravi realized whoever this Pyre was, he meant a great deal to her. He couldn't help but wonder if there would come a day when Taja's face would show such happiness at the mention of *his* name. "I don't know who it is, all I know is I need to get you to the main entrance. Now hurry!"

She followed willingly as he led the way. Most of the doors along the corridor were open, the rooms empty. The lab, when they passed through it, was empty as well. There was broken glass on the floor and various liquids spilled on the tables. Whoever had left the lab, left in a hurry. Twice, when they entered the next series of hallways, Ravi pulled her into a doorway to let armed guards pass. No one stopped them though.

"Is that smoke I smell?"

"Yes. The compound is on fire."

Rayne stopped suddenly. "But . . . what about the others? Won't they be trapped? It's our duty, with our gift of water, to help them."

"They're not trapped." He grabbed her arm and dragged her forward. "There are tunnels that go far back into the mountain. Almost everyone is already living inside the mountain, it's just you and the rest of the outsiders who were being kept in the forward part."

"The others!" She tried to pull away from him. "We have to go back."

"They're being taken care of." His voice was a little sharper than he'd intended. While part of him knew he was being unreasonable, he wished she would just shut up and trust him. "They're probably already at the entrance. It's not much further."

He was filled with a sudden sense of urgency. *Nereida, where are you?*

The fact that she hesitated before answering was not a good sign. But there was no lying mind to mind and she could not hide her fear.

I *am still in my room. They have locked us in.*

Ravi stopped in his tracks. *Rayne can manage on her own -- I'm coming for you.*

No*! You must get Rayne to safety first. She is* -- The rest of what she was about to tell him was cut off by an explosion in the corridor behind them.

Chapter Eighteen

From Nereida's Journal:

Perhaps Kaine has some small gift of foresight of his own, that is the only explanation I can find for him being in the M-class section when the explosion occurred. At the time all I could think of was how foolish he was, allowing himself to be trapped with us. Worse, we were not even trapped together. Most of us were in our rooms when the locks engaged. But Kaine was armed - it seemed prudent as he left his quarters and it turned out to be fortuitous as well. There being no need for caution, he blasted the locks on our doors to free us. However, his weapon had no effect on the heavy security door to our section.

Then there was a second explosion and I knew we would not have to worry about escape for us that way. Fissures opened up in the wall of the common room and I cannot explain it, but I somehow knew which one of them was the safest to traverse

The force of the explosion behind them threw them to the ground. As the debris began to settle, Ravi helped Rayne to her feet.

"Are you all right?" he asked, shouting to make himself heard over the noise.

"I think so," she shouted back. "How about you?"

"I'm fine. Look, just follow this passage until you reach an intersection. Stay to the right and it'll take you right to the entrance."

"Wait!" She grabbed his arm as he turned to go back the way they'd come from. "What are you doing? Aren't you coming with me?"

"I can't, there's someone else still trapped in there. Look, I don't have time to explain. Just get to the main entrance. There'll be a guard there, her name is Taja. She's one of the ones sent to rescue you and the others. Tell her . . . tell her I'm sorry."

He jerked himself free of her hold and raced back down the corridor. Rayne stared at his retreating figure for a moment, biting her lip in indecision. A rumbling sound filled the air and the ground under her feet shook slightly. The dust and smoke began to thicken. Self-preservation won out and she fled forward towards freedom.

The intersection of the corridors wasn't too far beyond where they'd stopped and she took the right branch, as instructed. She'd only gone a few yards when she could smell fresh air. The tantalizing scent led her to an open space, a foyer of sorts, with an open door beyond. Someone was pacing to and fro in front of the door, stopping when Rayne emerged from the hallway.

"Are you Taja?" Rayne asked tentatively, poised to run.

"You must be Rayne," the woman said with obvious relief. "The others are already out there. We need to hurry before—" she looked around, peering through the smoke. "Wait a minute. Where's Ravi?"

"He went back, something about someone else who needed saving," Rayne told her. "He said to tell you he's sorry."

"Damn him!" Taja swore violently.

The ground shook, throwing them off balance.

"Look, just go through this door and then straight through the gates to the ridge. The others will be waiting for you there."

"What about you?" Rayne asked, though she might just as well have saved her breath. The look on the guardswoman's face told her everything she needed to know.

"I have to go after him," Taja said.

"I understand," Rayne told her. "Good luck!"

She watched as Taja disappeared back down the smoke-filled corridor, and then turned towards the main door . . . and freedom

* * * * *

The further towards the M-section Ravi went, the worse the smoke was. His eyes stung and he held one arm across his mouth to keep from inhaling too much of it. The temperature was starting to rise.

Nereida, are you all right? Nereida!

There was no answer, but he did not get the sense she was dead.

The quarters for the M class were set back in the mountain with the others, down a corridor that ran parallel to the mountain. Ravi made his way towards the corridor, the dust and smoke so thick he could hardly see, until suddenly he was stopped. The way was blocked with debris. Frantically, he started clawing at the rubble.

Nereida!

This time there he could sense a flicker of her emotions.

Nereida, are you all right?

Kairavini? What has happened?

There was an explosion - I came as quickly as I could but the way is blocked.

He heard footsteps behind him and turned, unsurprised to see Taja emerge from the smoke.

"Taja is here with me," Ravi said aloud as well as mentally. "If we work together we can we can clear the passage."

No, Nereida told him. *There is no time. I know of another way, but you need to take care of the locks.*

He repeated what she said to Taja, then added, "How many others are trapped? It will be impossible to save them all."

"We need to get to the security office," Taja said. "There's a master control there for the door locks."

Ravi relayed what was happening to Nereida as he and Taja ran back towards the labs. He was a little surprised that there were no guards around, but then realized that those who had not been confined would have escaped through the main doors already. If they had any sense.

Taja halted at the door to the security office. "The bastards locked this one as well." Frustration filled her voice.

"Here, let me." Ravi pushed her gently to one side and had the lock open in seconds.

"You'll have to teach me how you do that."

"It would be my pleasure . . . if we survive."

She wasted no more time but went straight to the panel on the wall and tapped in the codes that released the locks throughout the compound. The override worked on everything but the heavy metal doors leading further back into the tunnels.

"That should do it," Taja said.

We are free, Nereida said. *I am leading those who are willing into the tunnels now.*

We'll come back and meet you, Ravi told her.

Go to the door leading into the mountain, the one you use to go exploring. Hurry, my brother!

As they left the security office, they ran into several guards who had gathered in the corridor nearby.

"What's happening? Where is everyone? Why were we locked in?"

Taja took a deep breath and immediately started to cough as the smoke-laden air filled her lungs. When she could speak she said, "We have been betrayed by Arjun. The mountain is on the verge of erupting and he has moved the rest of his compound elsewhere, leaving those he chooses not to take with him to die."

Voices raised in anger, overlapping with questions. Taja raised her hands for silence.

"We weren't the only ones left behind. I need your help to get the others to safety."

"Why should we help you?" one of the men asked. "I say we save ourselves."

This time the voices rose in assent.

Taja drew herself up proudly. "I am Taja Windsinger, of the Ardraci Black Ops. Any one of you who helps is guaranteed immunity. You have my word."

Six of the guards shook their heads and disappeared into the smoke. The remaining five stood their ground. "What do we need to do?"

"Some of the Breeders and Seeders were left behind as well. They'll be in the rooms marked with red. See if you can persuade them to leave their rooms - they'll die if they stay."

"What will you be doing?"

"We'll be doing the same, down the second corridor. We'll meet up at the security door leading into the mountain. We have a group coming from the M-section as well."

Another tremor shook the ground under their feet.

"Once we're all together we'll meet up at the main entrance. I have people on the outside waiting to help."

Kairavini, you need to move from that place.

What? Why?

You are in great danger! Move back towards the breeding quarters - hurry!

"Nereida says we need to get out of here," he said, grabbing Taja by the hand and dragging her along with him up the corridor.

"Come on everyone," she called over her shoulder. "This way."

Two of the guards looked at each other and then headed in the opposite direction. The rest followed Taja and Ravi. They'd just cleared the labs and were in the corridor to the breeding quarters when there was a series of small explosions behind them.

"What the hell was that?" one of the guards asked.

"It wasn't natural, that's for damn sure."

"It's as you said," Ravi said quietly to Taja. "Arjun never intended for those left behind to survive. He's cut us off from the main entrance."

"There must be a way," she argued. "Otherwise why go to the trouble of locking everyone in? We need to hurry."

The breeding quarters were divided into two sections, one for Breeders and one for Seeders. Taja and Ravi took the Breeders section, the three guards took the other. Taja pounded on the first door with red markings she came to but the woman on the other side refused to open it.

"How can I make you understand?" Taja asked. "If you stay in there you will die."

"Better death than betrayal of my place in the Program."

"What is wrong with these people?" she asked Ravi in despair.

He put an arm around her and pulled her gently away from the door. "We can't force her to leave if she's not willing. We'll try another door."

In all, only seven could be persuaded to leave the comfort and familiarity of their quarters. When they met up with the guards at the end of the section, there were another nine added to the total.

Hurry! Nereida said forcefully in Ravi's mind.

He winced. *We're almost there.*

"Nereida says --"

He was cut off as there the earth trembled beneath their feet, subsiding into tremors.

"We've got to get out of here," one of the guards shouted.

"That's what we're trying to do," Taja replied.
"We--"

There was a roaring noise and the earth heaved
under them, knocking them to the ground.

Chapter Nineteen

From Nereida's Journal:

Lies and more lies. I had never lied to my brother before, and now the lies were piling one on top of another. Letting him believe we were locked in was necessary to get him to disengage all of the locks before it was too late. He would not have been persuaded to leave me otherwise we had no time for explanations. I allowed him to believe we would meet on the other side of the security door because I knew that was the only way that had a chance of them surviving. My vision fractured, split into all the different possibilities and outcomes. Thoughts and images were coming so fast it was near to impossible to make sense of them all. Danger - that was the clearest of all. We were all in terrible danger. And there was only more to come. And so I told him what he needed to hear to move him in the right direction. Had he been thinking clearly, he would have known it too.

Taja groaned and tried not to inhale any more dust and ash than absolutely necessary. She tried to get up but she seemed to be pinned in place. There was something heavy, someone heavy, on top of her. Ravi had cushioned her fall as best he could, and then protected her with his body.

"Ravi." She choked and tried again, louder. "Kairavini, move. We have to get out of here."

He stirred and groaned.

Taja bit down on the E.T.T. to activate it.

You missed your rendezvous, the disembodied voice told her.

No kidding! We--wait. You're not my regular contact. What's going on?

My name is E.Z. I am in charge of the rescue operation.

Ravi finally moved enough she could slide out from under him. "Are you all right?" she asked.

It is to be hoped that you are within the outer section of the compound, E.Z.'s voice continued.

"I will be fine in a moment," Ravi said.

Taja rose to a kneeling position and started to check him over for injuries. The others were starting to sit up as well, talking to each other, a few crying.

No, we're at the far end of the living quarters, Taja told her new contact. *We're meeting up with another group and then heading back to the entrance.*

You will not get out that way.

Ravi clutched her hands in his. "As much as I enjoy your hands on me, it is not necessary. I am fine.

Just a few bruises." With Taja's help he sat up. "We need to get moving."

"Check on the others," she told him. "I'll just be a minute."

What do you mean we won't get out that way? she asked E.Z. *What other way is there?* Though the temperature in the corridor was steadily rising, she felt a chill at the thought of being trapped inside the mountain.

The small explosions you felt a short time ago were set by Dr. Arjun.

Damn him! He wanted to make sure none of the Breeders or Seeders escaped from the compound.

Indeed, E.Z. confirmed. *You will need to find your way through the mountain using the tunnel system.*

Are you insane? The volcano just erupted!

It was just a minor eruption and we are attempting to control it. The Elementals with you have little training, but they are powerful - they should be enough to keep you safe. But you will need to disable their inhibitors.

Taja looked towards where Ravi was helping the others to their feet. The dust was thick in the corridor and the heat was becoming unbearable.

I've only seen one person wearing an inhibitor--

Kairavini is a special case. The others had their inhibitors implanted just after reaching tespiro. Set your com link to a frequency of six-two-two-seven and give each elemental a short burst to the temple. There will be a brief discomfort, and then their gifts will be at full power.

Taja was outraged at the thought of inhibitors implanted in these people without their knowledge. *What about Ravi?*

His wristband will need to be removed. I suggest you hurry.

Wait! How are we supposed to get through the cave system.

There is one among you who knows the way. With that, the voice vanished.

"Damn, cryptic Illezie," Taja muttered.

Ravi joined her. "Two were killed by falling debris but the rest just have minor injuries. What do we do next?"

He seemed to have no problem with her in charge, for which Taja was very grateful. The task ahead would be difficult enough without having to deal with a male ego. "Let's get through that security door and meet up with your sister's group." She'd worry about disabling the inhibitors once they were all together.

They made their way as quickly as possible to the heavy metal door. Taja laid her hand on the surface and was relieved that it was not hot to the touch.

"All right, Ravi. Time for you to--"

One of the women at the back of the group suddenly screamed in fear.

"What is it?" Taja demanded. She fought her way through the group as it surged towards the door.

"By the gods!" She stood and stared, mesmerized by the bright river of lava inching slowly towards them. "Kairavini, hurry with that door!"

"I have it unlocked, but it's--" his voice broke off as he came up beside her. "The people we left behind . . ."

"We can't think about that now," Taja said, grabbing his arm. "We need to get out of here, now!"

"That's what I was about to tell you," he said, not budging. "The door's unlocked, but it's stuck. One of the tremors must have damaged the door frame."

They were forced to move back a few steps, away from the heat.

"Maybe if we get Nereida's group to push from the other side while we pull . . ."

Nereida, how close are you to the inner chamber?

I do not know, Ravi. We have had to make detours to avoid poisonous gasses and lava streams. We are close, I think.

Are you all right? Your voice in my head is weak.

It is interference from the rock. Your voice is weak as well. Where are you?

We are still on the other side of the door, but we will be through momentarily, he hastened to assure her.

Hurry, brother! You must be on the other side of the door before the volcano erupts!

We will be.

"I don't think we can count on their help," he told Taja. "They have yet to reach the inner chamber."

"Damn!" She paced from one side of the corridor to the other. "All right. Let me see how bad the door is."

They returned to the panicky group milling around the door. The handle of the door was not large enough to accommodate more than one pair of hands at a time and the three guards were taking turns trying to pull it open. They were having very little success.

"If we had something to pry it open with . . ." one of the guards said.

"All right, you three see if you can find anything useful back that way," Taja ordered, pointing away from the lava flow. "Ravi, let's see if we can do something about that lava."

"What about the rest of us," one of the Seeders called angrily. "Did you lead us here just so we could die?"

"No one's going to die. Look, I know you don't know me, but I need you to trust me. I'm here to help. We're going to get out of this."

"You would already be dead, had we not persuaded you from your rooms," Ravi pointed out.

Taja shook her head and pulled him away. "We're wasting time, arguing. We have to stop that lava."

"I agree, but how do you propose we do so?"

"Not we," she said, coming to a stop as close as she dared to the flow, "You."

"Me?" Ravi looked at her in surprise. "What can I do?"

"You're a Water Elemental, there's got to be some way of drawing enough water here to halt that lava."

Ravi looked at the oncoming stream, brow furrowed. He vaguely remembered his lessons and how they were shown how to pull water molecules from the air around them. "Without the enhancer we had for our lessons, I fear the amount of water I can draw to me will be far from sufficient to do any good."

"I thought we already talked about this. Just like everything else about this place, you were lied to about your gift. Ravi, you're the most powerful Water Elemental ever born."

Ravi was shaking his head before she'd even finished. "I know you would like me to think so, but there is no reason for you to stroke my ego."

"I'm not stroking your ego. Every last one of the participants in the Program has been fitted with an inhibitor. It prevents you from reaching your full potential."

"You mentioned an inhibitor before. You said it was in my wristband. But no one else wears such a band."

"That's because no one else needs to. Theirs were implanted directly into their heads. But you were so powerful that your body rejected the inhibitor, so they had to make a special one for you. It was probably your body rejecting the inhibitor that gave you severe headaches, they just let you believe the external inhibitor was preventing them."

The lava continued to inch forward. Taja reached for the knife in her boot sheath. "Do you trust me Ravi?"

"You know I do," he replied.

"Then trust me in this. Give me your hand."

Without hesitation he placed his hand, the one with the band around the wrist, in hers. She carefully slipped the point of the knife under the band and began sawing through the tough material. There was a small spark as she cut through a wire, then with a flick of her wrist she was through. She had to pull the band away from Ravi's wrist, there were several filaments from the band imbedded in his skin.

Ravi's eyes widened as Taja tossed the band aside. Sinking to his knees, his hands went to his head and he gasped as his full elemental power descended upon him.

Taja was kneeling beside him when one of the guards came rushing back.

"We found this," he said, holding out an iron bar.

"Perfect," she told him. "See if you can start prying the door open. You can get some of the others to help."

"What's wrong with him?" he asked, nodding towards Ravi. He took a step back as he noticed the water seeping into the ground around them. "He's returning to his element!"

"He's fine!" Taja said fiercely. "Just worry about getting that door open."

The look he shot her before he turned and hurried away was full of pity.

Ravi struggled for control as the full weight of his power surged through him. He was hyper aware of the water all around him and fought to keep the water molecules within from tearing him apart. The water called to him - from the air, from the rock, from the woman beside him . . .

Taja! He turned his focus to her hands on his face as she turned his head towards her, on the words she was saying.

"Remember your lessons," she was telling him. He felt the shudder that ran through her at the feel of the cool dampness of his skin under her hands. "If you do not master your element, it will master you."

"I . . . I remember." He took several deep breaths.

He could do this. He was the master here, not his element. If he lost control there would be nothing left of him but a puddle at Taja's feet. He would never know the feel of freedom, or the sun on his face, or what it would be like spending his life loving one person. He could do this.

"Remember how you were taught to draw the water to you," Taja said, helping him to his feet again.

"It's just--it's just so much," he said. "I feel . . . I don't know what I feel. I've never felt anything like it."

"I daresay it will take some getting used to, and I wish we were able to gradually reduce the effects of the inhibitor, but you need to stop that lava."

Ravi took another shuddering breath and turned towards the fiery stream inching towards them. "I can do this."

He could feel the water in the air, in the rock, there was even a kind of moisture in the lava itself that changed the rock from a solid to a liquid state. He remembered clearly the lesson in the cave where he and his classmates created balls of water.

Closing his eyes, he sent his awareness into the rock around them, seeking out the water molecules and drawing them forward. He did not need to hear Taja's sharp intake of breath to know it was working, he could feel the water gathering between them and the lava. Remembering how difficult it had been to gather enough water to satisfy the instructor during his lessons, he sent his awareness further, recognizing water trapped in small pockets in the rock, gathering it to him.

Taja's hand on his arm startled his eyes open. He lost control of the wall of water he'd created and it collapsed - both on the lava stream and on them. The lava hissed as steam boiled upwards, but a black crust formed where the water struck it.

"I did it!" It was so incredibly easy, once he was able to control the pull of his element.

He hugged a drenched Taja to him and she hugged him back. She kissed him and said, "I never doubted for a moment you couldn't. Although I did wonder if you meant to drown us with the amount of water you drew in."

"I'm sorry," he said sheepishly. "I did that quite a lot during training as well - getting people wet, I mean. Let me see if I can fix it."

Releasing her, he stood back a step and then concentrated. Calling the excess moisture from Taja's clothing was actually more difficult than pulling the water from the air and rock around them. It needed a far more delicate touch but when he was finished her clothes were dry once more.

"How did you do that?" she asked in amazement.

"I wasn't sure I could," he admitted. "I remember being told during training that we should be able to pull the water out of anything around us."

He grinned like a child with a new toy as he dried himself off. He would have liked nothing better than to be able to explore his new found gift further, but it would have to wait.

"Do you think it will hold?" he asked, looking towards the brittle looking rock holding back the lava. It was still hard to believe it worked.

"I think so," Taja said. "It should at least hold long enough for us to get through that door. C'mon, let's see how they're doing."

Together they went back to the security door, just in time to see one the guardsman finally pulling the door open enough that he could get the pry bar in. With the help of two of the Seeders, he began forcing the door open.

"It just needs to be open enough for us to pass through," Taja told them. "We've dealt with the lava for now, but I don't know how long it will hold."

With renewed vigor, the men pulled at the pry bar, forcing the door open just enough for people to squeeze through, one at a time.

When everyone was gathered in the large chamber, the guard tossed the bar to the side and asked, "What do we do now?"

"First we need to get that door shut again," Ravi said. As proud as he was of his accomplishment, he wasn't arrogant enough to believe the barrier would hold for long.

"And then," Taja said to the breeding group, "I'm going to activate your elemental powers."

There was a noise from the corridor behind the door and Ravi looked back through to see that the lava had continued to build up behind the barrier he'd made and was now spilling over.

"Someone help me with this."

Together he and one of the other Seeders grabbed a hold of the door and pulled it shut again. The lock clicked into place and he breathed a sigh of relief.

"That should hold for now, but we need to get moving as soon as possible. There's no telling how many other fissures have opened up," he said.

N*ereida. We are in the larger chamber now. The security door is closed behind us but there is a lava flow in the corridor on the other side. Nereida?*

Her mind's voice, when it came, was faint. *We should be joining you shortly, brother. Several of us are injured and we are moving slowly.*

A*re you all right?*

I *am fine. But it is becoming difficult to communicate this way.*

W*e'll wait for you here.*

* * * * *

"What did you mean when you said you would activate our elemental powers?" one of the women asked Taja. "Our power, such as it is, has been active since we passed our *tespiro*."

"That's true," Taja agreed, "but it's not the whole story. Once the danger of *tespiro* was over, you had an inhibitor implanted to suppress your power."

"But we needed an enhancer in order to learn to control our element," one of the men protested. "Our gifts weren't strong enough to need to be suppressed."

"That is what I believed as well." Ravi came over to stand beside her, offering his support. "But it was a lie. My gift is strong enough that the implant wouldn't work, so I was fitted with a cuff." He held up his arm so they could see the red band around his wrist where the cuff had chaffed. "Now that it is gone I am able to do this."

He began to pull water out of the air around him and once he had a ball the size of his head he made it dance in the air in front of them. It elongated and shrank, went through a series of geometric shapes, and with a final flourish rained down harmlessly to be reabsorbed into the ground.

"If we're going to get out of this alive, we'll need all your gifts before we're done. Who wants to have theirs activated first?"

The man who protested stepped forward. Ravi watched curiously as Taja removed the com-link from her wrist, then adjusted a setting on it. She placed it against the man's temple and pressed a button.

The man gave a start, then his eyes widened. "I can feel it! I can feel my element!"

A sudden wind swept through the cavern. "I did that!" he said excitedly.

Taja grinned and turned to Ravi. "I think this is going to take a while. I'm sure you know this cavern better than anyone, why don't you take the guards and see if you can find some supplies? If we're going to get out of here alive we'll need food and water."

He caught her arm as she was about to turn away and pulled her toward him for a quick kiss. "There is no if about it. We *will* get out of here alive."

She blushed as she turned back to the Elementals, who were staring in shock at the sight of a Seeder kissing a guard. Ravi felt a flash of masculine satisfaction. Things were different now and they might as well start getting used to it.

He led the guards to the main storeroom where the crates of supplies had been stacked and catalogued. In short order they had portable lights, blankets, and a large supply of dried rations.

As an afterthought Ravi added containers for water. Although there was a large supply of water in one of the store rooms, they had no need to weigh themselves down with it. He and the other three Water Elementals could pull all the water they needed out of the air.

Kairavini! Something is happening!

Nereida's mind voice hit him like a fist and he staggered. *What is it?*

The heat from the volcano is evaporating. But it is wrong . . . her mind voice was almost a moan.

"Ravi! What's wrong?" Taja rushed up to him as he made it back to the cavern, dropping the supplies he was carrying.

"I'm not sure. Have you noticed it getting cooler in here?"

"I thought it was my imagination."

She shivered and he put an arm around her, as much for comfort as for warmth. "It's not. Nereida said there's something's wrong."

The ground began to tremble beneath their feet. A quivering that rippled through the cavern.

Is it the volcano erupting?

No, Nereida said, her mind voice a mere thread. *It is something much worse.*

Chapter Twenty

From Nereida's Journal:

Images came and went so quickly it was like seeing through more than one set of eyes simultaneously. I could see outside of the compound, the small group standing on the ridge and the man below, standing in a column of flame. I could see those who travelled with me and all the possibilities before them. I could see Dr. Arjun and those he'd chosen, and the realization of what he'd done come over the ones he saved. I felt only the smallest sense of satisfaction in knowing that even should none of us survive, neither would Arjun's breeding program. And I could see my brother and his group, safe for now. The visions were weakening me to the point where mind-to-mind communication was all but impossible. But I needed only one more lie to my brother to get him moving in the right direction.

The artificial lights in the cavern flickered and went out. There were a few gasps, but the guard who'd found the portable lights had the presence of mind to start turning the lights on and passing them out. The ground continued to shake and dust and debris began raining down on them from above.

"We need to leave this place before we're trapped!" one of the Breeders called out.

Other voices rose in assent.

Nereida, what is happening? Ravi asked desperately.

There is a Fire Elemental on the outside. Just as you are able to draw water out of the air, he is able to draw the heat from the volcano to keep it from erupting. Her mind's voice was just a whisper.

But if the danger has passed, why does the earth still shake?

He is not in control of his Element. He takes too much--

The ground heaved beneath their feet and the air grew suddenly colder. Ravi could see his breath by the glow of his hand held light.

My brother, you must leave without us if you are to survive.

What? No! I will not leave without you!

We are further inside the mountain than you and the way to the storage cavern is blocked.

We have Earth Elementals who can clear the way--

It is too dangerous, the mountain is too unstable.

But--

Do not fear for us, we have another way that is much safer. You and the others must take the tunnel that leads past the training caverns, and then follow your heart.

Promise me I will see you on the other side.

I--

Promise me!

I . . . promise. And with that her mind's voice faded completely.

Nereida? Nereida!

Taja placed her hand on his arm. "What's happening?"

"Nereida says the tremors are being caused by a Fire Elemental on the outside who's pulled too much of the heat from the volcano." Why had her mind's voice been so weak? He had the nagging feeling that something was not right with his sister.

"I didn't know that was possible," Taja said in surprise.

"Nor did I," he admitted. "Nereida's group will not be joining us after all. She claims the way is blocked."

"Oh, no!" Her grip tightened on his arm.

"She also says they have another way out, safer than ours."

"Do you believe her?"

Did he? He had no choice really. But there was a troubled look on his face as he said, "Yes, I do."

"But?" she prompted.

"I can't help feeling she is holding something back." He sighed and shook his head. "But I cannot dwell on it, right now we need to get moving."

"Yes, but which way?" Taja asked. "My contact assured me there's someone who knows the way, I'd assumed it was Nereida. Without her, how will we know where to go?"

"That way," Ravi told her, pointing towards the tunnel.

"How do you know? Did you find a map after all?"

"Nereida told me. Sometimes she . . . sees things."

The gift of foresight was very rare amongst the Ardraci, but it did happen."All right then," she said briskly. Still holding his hand, she moved to the front of the group.

"Listen up everyone. The cold is just temporary and already the tremors are subsiding. The danger from the volcano is over, but we still have to get out of here."

"But how?" one of the Breeders asked in a tearful voice. "The way is blocked."

"This mountain is riddled with caves and passages," Ravi said. "We will use them to escape to the other side."

"Which one of you has the map?" a Seeder called out. "Can we make copies in case we're separated?"

"There is no map," Taja said. Anything else she might have added was drowned out by a chorus of angry voices.

"Then how will you know which way to go?" came the angry demand. "We could wander these caverns for weeks until we run out of supplies and starve to death!"

"Quiet! All of you!" Ravi bellowed. He waited until the heated protests died down before continuing. "I know which way to go."

"And why should we trust you?"

"Because your other choice," Taja told them grimly, "Is to stay here."

The three guards divided up the rations and water bottles, making bundles of them with the blankets. The dried rations were already conveniently made up into packets and several packets were included in each pile. Every person got a blanket wrapped bundle along with a portable light.

Clasping Taja's hand in his, Ravi stepped forward with far more confidence than he was feeling. They had the others pair up, suggesting that only one light per pair be used. There was no way of knowing how far they had to travel and they needed to conserve the power in the lights.

He felt a pang as they passed the turn-off for the tunnel to the grotto where he and Taja had made love. It had only been a few days but it felt like a lifetime ago. Taja's hand tightened fractionally on his and he glanced over to see her smiling at him.

"Do you think they'd mind waiting here while we made a little side trip?" he asked.

Her smile blossomed into a grin. "It's a nice idea, but I want our next time to be in a proper bed."

Chuckling softly he gave her hand a squeeze, and then turned his full attention on where they were going. The tunnel twisted and wound its way onward, sometimes narrowing so that they were forced to walk in single file, sometimes widening to the point where Ravi had Taja turn on her light as well to make sure they were going in the right direction. After several hours, Taja called a halt when they reached a place where the tunnel opened up into a wide cavern.

"What's happening? Why are we stopping?"

She waited patiently for the voices to die down before speaking.

"There's no problem, I just thought we could all use a rest. This seems like as good a place as any for a break. I want everyone to have something to eat and drink, and then we'll try and get some sleep. Ravi? Could you and the other Water Elementals fill everyone's water bottles?"

"Of course." Ravi felt a thrill at the opportunity to exercise his elemental power. Unfortunately, no matter how hard he concentrated he kept overfilling the bottles and giving the people holding them a good wetting in the process.

After the third time this happened, he said to Taja, "It's so frustrating! I don't understand why I can drench a lava stream but can't fill a simple water bottle."

"I think," Taja told him, "the problem is that your element is too strong for such a small task."

Ravi heaved a sigh. "Maybe I should just dig a hole to fill with water."

"I have a better idea."

He watched, baffled, as she gathered up half a dozen water bottles and placed them in a group in front of him.

"Okay, now fill them," she told him.

Shrugging, he narrowed his eyes and concentrated. The first bottle began to fill with water and then toppled over as water began gushing out of it.

"Sorry," he said. "I just can't seem to control the flow rate."

Taja picked up the bottle and set it up right again. "Try again. But this time, try filling all the bottles at the same time."

With a sigh Ravi tried again. This time instead of concentrating on one bottle, he concentrated on the whole group. In seconds all six bottles were filled with only a slight spillage. He turned to Taja in surprise.

"How did you know that would work?"

"I didn't. It just seemed logical that your gift is so powerful that it needed a larger outlet."

He pulled her in for a kiss and said, "Not only beautiful, but wise as well."

"And don't you forget it!" she said with a laugh."Now let's find someplace to sit."

While the air around them was still cooler than it should be, it was not uncomfortably so. Lights flashed around the cavern as the group spread out to find comfortable places to rest. Or at least as comfortable as possible. There was very little ground cover over the bare rock.

Ravi and Taja sat together with their backs to the rough stone of one of the cavern's walls and shared a ration pack.

"Are you able to speak to your sister yet?" Taja asked.

He tried reaching out mentally for Nereida but there was no response. "No. I would not worry but she seemed so weak earlier."

Taja hesitated, then said, "My grandmother had visions, but they often left her weak. Perhaps she is just conserving her strength."

"I never thought of that," he admitted. The more he thought of it, though, the more plausible it sounded. He remembered Nereida's pallor the few times she had a vision while she was with him. And twice she'd had nose bleeds.

"I think there's something in all this rock that's interfering," she added, resting her head on his shoulder. "I lost contact with my people back at the security door."

Ravi pulled one of the blankets over them. "Perhaps that is why I cannot reach her," he said, though there was doubt in his voice.

There was no response from Taja. She was sound asleep.

The timer on Taja's communication wristband chimed after they'd been resting for three hours. There were grumbles and protests, but the group gathered in the centre of the cavern again.

"I'm sorry everyone," Taja told them. "I know you're tired, so am I, but we need to keep moving. We don't know what's going on outside the mountain or if the danger inside has passed."

The security guards had moved forward to check the path ahead, and one of them came hurrying back. "We have a problem," he said.

Taja rubbed her forehead where a headache was starting and sighed. "What is it?"

"The path splits into three at the edge of this chamber."

She stared at him as voices erupted around them. Ravi followed in her wake as she moved towards where the other guards were waiting. The chamber narrowed slightly before splitting into three separate branches - two close together and one further apart.

"We went several feet down each one and there's no indication they join up again," the guard said.

"So which one do we take?"

Like an echo, Ravi heard Nereida's voice telling him to follow his heart. "We take the left branch," he said firmly.

"Are you sure?" Taja asked, glancing over at him.

"Positive."

The left tunnel started out wider than the others, but after they'd been following it for a while it started to narrow. Ravi couldn't help feeling somewhat apprehensive. What if he was wrong? What if he had misinterpreted what Nereida told him?

They were walking single file when they came to another split and without hesitation he led everyone to the left. He had to trust that he was doing the right thing. Still, he breathed easier once the tunnel began to widen again.

Even with the lights the darkness was oppressive. They passed through several smaller caves and when they came to the shore of a small, underground lake, Taja called a halt so they could rest again.

"I wish there was some way to tell how far we have to go," she said to Ravi.

"I am still unable to speak with Nereida. Are you able to make contact to the outside yet?"

She shook her head. "No, but that doesn't really tell me anything."

Ravi stared thoughtfully into the darkness. "There hasn't been any tremors since we left the storage chamber. Perhaps . . ."

"Perhaps what?"

He got to his feet to address the group at large. "Which one of you is the highest rated Earth Elemental?"

There was a murmur of voices and then a short, stocky woman stood up. "I am."

"I remember when I training, I was able to sense a great body of water connected to the small one in the training chamber. Is it possible for you to sense how close we are to the end of our journey?"

"I-I-I don't know. Being able to use my ability is very new to me."

"Would you be willing to try?" Taja came over to stand by Ravi's side. "Where I come from, Earth Elementals are able to sense many things about the earth around them."

"We were never trained in such a thing," the woman said with a frown. "I don't know if it will work. But I'm willing to try."

She stood up straight, a look of intense concentration on her face, and closed her eyes. After a few seconds, beads of sweat dotted her face. The ground around them began to tremble and she opened her eyes with a gasp.

"I'm sorry, I didn't mean to do that!" She took several deep breaths. "There is so much earth all around us, it is hard to get any sense of where it ends. I could sense gaps in the earth, caves like the one we're in now, but small ones."

"No sense of a large space?" Ravi asked.

She shook her head. "No, I'm sorry. Would you like me to try again?"

"No," he told her. "I don't think we should risk it. The volcano might still be unstable - we don't want to set it off again."

"Thank you for trying," Taja told her.

The woman nodded and returned to her place.

"All right, everyone," Taja said. "We'll rest for another half hour and then move on."

Chapter Twenty-One

From Nereida's Journal:

There were times, as we made our way through the mountain, when I did not believe I would make it to the other side. As I have already said, I never fully regained my health after tespiro and the visions have taken a heavy toll on me.

While I lied to Ravi about so many things, I did not lie when I said we were already further inside the mountain. This was by virtue of where we started. The M-section was already deeper in the mountain than the rest of the compound. The fissure that opened up in the common room opened up to a honey comb of tunnels - lava chutes from previous eruptions, natural caves, and vents filled with gas. But it was not noxious fumes and lava streams that impeded our progress, it was my weakness. I would tell Kaine which way to go, but there was always a wait time while I regained consciousness before we could journey from that point.

It felt like they'd been traversing the tunnels for days, but Ravi knew it couldn't be more than twenty-four hours. He also knew all he had to do was ask Taja and she'd be able to tell him the exact amount of time, right down to the minute using the time piece she wore, but he decided he'd rather not know. There was something else on his mind.

"What happens when we come to the end of our journey?" he asked.

"What?" Taja stumbled and he reached out to steady her.

"What will become of us, all of us from the Program, when we reach the ... outside?"

"As soon as we're within range I'll contact my team and they'll meet us. After that ... I haven't really thought that far ahead, to be honest. The focus has always been on getting as many as possible out, not what happens after that."

He nodded thoughtfully.

"There will be questions to be answered," Taja continued, after a few moments. "And I would imagine anyone wishing it will be taken to Ardraci to start a new life."

Ravi lapsed into silence again, too unsure of himself, of them, to ask what he really wanted to know. What was going to happen to the two of them. Would they part ways, he to a new life on Ardraci and Taja back to her old life? Would he ever see her again?

Or would they build on the closeness they shared, starting a life together? This jumble of feelings was still too new for him to be sure of anything, other than he could not imagine his life without Taja in it.

He glanced over at her but she appeared to be lost in thought as well - he couldn't help but wonder what she was thinking. Whatever it was, there was a serious expression on her face.

"Tell me about the outside," he said, not liking the silence between them.

"I don't know where to start," she said with a rueful laugh.

"I've seen pictures," he told her. "Many years ago my friend Zephryn got a hold of an illicit data cube that had information about other worlds. I saw lakes and forests and vast plains, in some places there were all three at once."

Taja nodded. "The world we're on right now has all those things. If I remember the map of this area correctly, we should be exiting the volcano near the shore of an ocean."

"That's a large body of water, is it not?"

"That's right. It's like - I don't know how to describe it." Her brow furrowed in thought.

"Is it bigger than the lake in the cavern?" he asked.

"Much bigger. So big it stretches to the horizon where it meets the sky." She gestured with her hands, holding them out from side to side.

"The sky," Ravi repeated. He couldn't suppress a shiver. "I do not know if I wish to see this sky. From what I could tell it is like a vast sea of nothingness."

Taja glanced over at him. "I never thought about it that way. To me the sky is always changing. Sometimes it's clear and so blue you feel like you could reach up and touch it."

"But it is not always bright, is this not so?"

"No, when the sun sets it becomes dark and the stars appear. It's a breathtaking sight."

"Stars ... they are the suns from faraway worlds. I admit I have a hard time picturing a sky full of suns."

"They're so small they just look like small sparks of light." Taja paused for a moment before continuing. "Think of being in one of the caverns we've passed through, only there's tiny points of light in the ceiling above us. That's what night is like."

Ravi thought about the last cavern they were in and then tried to imagine points of light from the ceiling. It didn't seem so bad, but he still shivered again.

The beam from the light in his hand caught something in the tunnel ahead of them and suddenly all thoughts of the outside vanished from his mind.

"I was afraid of something like this," Taja said. "I'm actually surprised we didn't run into it sooner."

Dirt and rock filled the passage. There was no getting around it, it completely blocked the way.

"We have to find a way past this," Ravi said. "The way to the outside lies beyond this barrier - we have come too far to go back." Nereida had told him to follow his heart. His heart told him that if they went back they would never find their way out.

"I don't think we can dig our way out," Taja said, taking a closer look at the debris blocking the tunnel. It was almost like a solid wall of dirt and rock."This is packed pretty solid."

Voices rose from behind them, wanting to know why they were stopping. Taja turned to face the group, Ravi at her side.

"There's nothing to worry about," she assured everyone . "We knew this was a possibility when we started out, but it's nothing we can't overcome. Could I have the Earth Elementals at the front of the line?"

"Are you sure about this?" Ravi asked. "After what happened in the cavern ..."

"We don't have much choice."

The six Earth Elementals pushed their way to the front of the group. The woman who'd used her gift in the cavern where they'd stopped earlier seemed to be the spokeswoman for them.

"What is it? Is something wrong?"

"The passage is blocked," Taja told her, not mincing words. "We're hoping you and the other Earth Elementals can clear the way."

The woman looked past her, training her light on the earth and rock filling the passage. "We have never used our gifts in such a way. It is possible, in theory, but what if we only make matters worse?"

"I do not believe we have come this far only to die," Ravi said.

The woman spoke quietly with the other Earth Elementals and then turned back to Ravi and Taja. "We will do what we can. But I suggest everyone move back several yards, just in case."

"Agreed," Taja said. "You heard the lady," she said in a louder voice. "I need everyone to back up and give the Earth Elementals some room to work."

Amid much muttering and grumbling, the others did as requested. Ravi and Taja stood at the front of the group to watch the Earth Elementals at work.

After a quick consultation, the smaller group turned and faced the obstruction. At first nothing happened. Then a trickle of dirt slid from the top of the pile, snaking off towards the side of the passage. It was followed by a second trickle, then a rivulet of dirt.

The entire mound trembled but the passage around it stayed firm.

"Yes, that's the way," the leader of the Earth Elementals said. "Along the sides too, not just along the base."

Taja and Ravi watched in fascination as the earth flowed like water, taking the rocks and rubble with it as it moved along the floor and up the sides of the passage. When the earth stopped moving the passage was clear.

The Earth Elementals were grinning at each other in triumph. "We did it!" one of them said.

"Well done," Taja told them. "But we need to keep moving."

Basking in the praise they were receiving from the rest of the group, the Earth Elementals returned to their place in line and Taja and Ravi continued to guide the group forward. The path widened slightly, but the ceiling seemed lower and they were moving slightly downwards.

They travelled for about another hour before the passage opened up into another large cavern.

"All right, everyone," Taja said. "I think we could all use a break. No sleeping this time though. Make sure you have something to eat and drink to keep up your strength."

No one in the weary group argued. They spread out in the cavern and broke out the rations.

Taja joined Ravi at the far side of the cavern. "Here," she said, passing him a protein bar. "You need to eat too."

He took it from her without comment, chewing on it automatically. There was a sick feeling in the pit of his stomach as he played his light over the wall of the cavern. He shone the light to either side as well, just to be sure, and the sick feeling grew.

"What is it?" Taja asked, catching his mood.

The protein bar Ravi was eating felt like dust in his mouth. "There does not appear to be an exit from this chamber."

In each of the other caverns they had encountered throughout their journey there had always been a way out. Sometimes it was just a matter of following the path they were on directly across the chamber, sometimes there was more than one tunnel to choose from. But there was always an exit. Until now.

Taja's light played alongside of his over the rock face. "Are you sure? Maybe the tunnel's just off to the side."

One of the former guards joined them. "Is anything wrong?"

Ravi tuned out their voices as he stepped closer to the wall of the chamber. He panned his light slowly to the left, following in its wake for a closer inspection of the rock in front of him. Maybe the passage was just hidden.

Black rock, grey rock, earth - all combined with a smell he couldn't identify. He turned and went the other way but it was much the same, except the smell was not as strong.

By this time several others had joined Taja and the guard, and it was with great reluctance Ravi turned to face them. He'd failed. He'd let Taja down. He'd let everyone down. He'd been so cocksure that he knew what he was doing, where he was going, and now the whole group was going to have to pay the price for his arrogance.

"If there is a way out, it is not at this end of the cavern," Ravi told them.

"All right everyone," Taja's voice rose over the sudden swell of angry mutterings. "There's no reason to panic. I want everyone to spread out. Use your lights to check all around the perimeter. There may be tunnels off to the side."

Ravi watched the lights darting around the chamber as the others dispersed to search the chamber.

"It's not your fault," Taja said, suddenly at his side.

"I am the one who lead us here. You all trusted me."

"And I still trust you. We *will* find our way out."

He was about to answer when the group began forming around them again.

"We've searched the whole cavern," said the guard who seemed to be the spokesperson. "There doesn't seem to be any way out but the way we came in."

"All right," Taja said briskly. "Obviously we've taken a wrong turn somewhere and we need to re-trace our steps. We must have missed a tunnel somewhere."

Voices rose in anger and protest. Ravi couldn't blame them - it was a long way back to the last chamber and since they'd been moving steadily downhill, it would be all uphill.

"Enough!" Taja shouted. "Arguing isn't going to change our situation. Now, what we need to--"

"I think we've found something!" an older Seeder, Ravi thought it was one of the Earth Elementals, interrupted Taja. "Over here."

Ravi went with her as she followed the man back to the area where he'd noticed the strange smell. The woman who seemed to be the leader of the Earth Elementals was frowning at the wall.

"What is it?" Taja asked.

"Do you remember when you asked me about sensing the earth?" the woman asked.

Taja nodded.

"When I did so, I could sense nothing but the earth and what it contained. But I tried it here and . . . ." Her gaze went back to the wall.

"And?" Ravi prompted.

Looking back at him again she said, "This time when I reach out I can sense nothing but emptiness."

Taja was sniffing the air. "Do you smell that? I think that's . . . Ravi, can I get you to see if you can sense any water ahead?"

"What is it?"

She shook her head. "Just try it."

"All right." Turning to face the wall, he took a deep breath and pushed out with his senses. He must be getting better with practice because he was sensing so much more than before. Now he was aware of the moisture in the air of the cavern, the nervous sweat coating the bodies around them. He pushed forward and felt the molecules of water in the rock itself and beyond that --

His eyes widened. "It's incredible! I-I don't know how to describe it. There is more water beyond this wall than I have ever dreamed of."

"That's good," Taja said. "That's what I was hoping you'd find. Now I need an Air Elemental."

One of them pushed his way to the front of the crowd. "What would you have me do?"

"I need you to do just what the others did. See if you can sense air on the other side of this wall."

The man frowned, but this was soon replaced by a look of concentration. It took him longer than the others, but like Ravi his eyes were soon wide with shock. "It's endless! It-it's terrifying!"

"Thank you," Taja told him. "All right, all you Earth Elementals. I need you to break through this wall."

"No!" Ravi protested. She didn't know what she was doing. There was far too much water on the other side of that wall - they'd drown if it got in here.

"Trust me," she told him. "As I trusted in you, trust me in this."

He hesitated, then nodded, standing aside as the Earth Elementals used their power to open a hole in the wall in front of them. He was fully prepared to use his gift to prevent water from pouring into the chamber, but it wasn't necessary. As the Elementals broke through, air blew into the cavern carrying with it the scent he'd noticed before.

"Sea air," Taja told them, a smile on her face. "Welcome to the Outside, everyone."

Chapter Twenty-Two

From Nereida's Journal:

This accounting of my life was begun just before our exodus from the compound and ends with our journey's end. Kaine lends me his strength so that I may finish my story and Sta'at . . . she is a source of unimaginable comfort to me. I keep expecting her to depart, to find another whose body she may share, but she does not. I have asked her what will happen to her spirit should my body fail, as I know it will, but she does not answer. That in itself is my answer. I have had one last vision, and I must survive long enough to pass it on. But it is so hard to stay awake.

Taja's smile faltered as the only ones that moved forward were the three guards. "This is it, this is what we've been searching for," she said, gesturing towards the large hole the Earth Elementals had created.

Two of the guards stepped through the opening while the third hung back. "Good luck," he told her.

"What do you mean by that?" she demanded.

"These people have never been outside of the compound. While the thought of escaping to the outside might have kept them going, the reality of it might be more than they can accept." He gave her a sympathetic look and then he, too, went through the opening.

"He's right," Ravi said, coming up to stand beside her. "We were raised to fear the outside, to believe it is too dangerous for us to survive in. It was considered the severest of punishments, to be banished to the outside."

"Was anyone ever banished?"

He hesitated. "I remember, shortly after I recovered from my *tespiro* there was a pair who committed an unsanctioned breeding . . ."

"Unsanctioned breeding?"

"Any breeding activity that took place without approval from Dr. Arjun was considered unsanctioned." He smiled fleetingly at her. "One was air and one was earth - I can't remember which was which. But in any case, they were caught and their punishment was to be banished to the outside."

"But you don't think that's what happened," she guessed.

"Though there were a few accounts of sightings of them being taken to the main entrance, no one saw them at the actual gates. And that night I saw a group of six hooded figures being escorted towards the security door in the mountain. The next day we discovered some of the instructors were missing too."

"He probably had them killed and the bodies disposed of," Taja finished for him. She wondered how many people hired by Dr. Arjun were never seen again. Glancing over at the group, she saw that many of them had moved away from the cave's mouth and back inside.

What was she supposed to do with them? She tried to imagine what it would be like to have spent your whole life inside the mountain, without even a window to the outside. Never once feeling the grass under your feet or breathing in the summer scented air . . . It didn't bear thinking of.

She started as she felt Ravi's hand slip into hers. "I trust you," he said simply.

Tears pricked at her eyes. Her fingers tightened around his and together they moved towards the exit from the cave. As they stumbled over the threshold, she could feel a shiver run through him. Then they were through, standing on a gentle slope of grass that led down to a sandy beach.

"Look," she told him, nodding her head towards the sky. "Stars."

He looked upwards, eyes wide. They stared up at the stars for a few moments, then she tugged him forwards.

"C'mon," she said. "There's a lot more to see."

The breeze coming off the water was warm, and the waves lapped gently at the shore. One of the guards had started a small fire on the beach, and she could just make out the other two scavenging for driftwood. Ravi stopped the second his feet hit the sand, pulling free from her hold as he jumped back.

"What is this?"

"It's all right," Taja told him. "It's sand - particles of rock that have been worn down by wind and water. Just like in the grotto, only not as dense. It may slide around some under your feet, but it's perfectly safe to walk on."

She reached for his hand again. "What do you think of the outside so far?"

He hesitated for a long moment. "Is it always so dark?"

"No." She laughed and shook her head. "This is the night I told you about. By not for much longer. See that glow over there?" She pointed towards the right. "That's the sun coming up."

Ravi let go of her hand and moved closer to where the waves were racing onto the shore, then being drawn back into the ocean. He seemed mesmerized.

"Well," the cynical guard who'd wished her good luck said. "I see you got one of them out. Now only fifteen more to go."

"Give them time," she admonished. "Try and put yourself in their place and think what it must be like to be confronted by a whole world you never knew existed."

He snorted. "Maybe they'll all end up paralyzed by fear, like that one," he nodded towards Ravi, standing on the shore.

Taja frowned. She went over and put a hand on his arm to get his attention. "What is it?" she asked, worried when he kept staring off over the water.

"It's not right," he muttered.

"What's not right?" The worry ratcheted up a notch. "Ravi talk to me!"

"Out there," he said, gaze fixed on the horizon. "The water is . . . there is something very wrong with the water. It is as though it is angry."

"Angry?" Her brow furrowed as she turned to watch as well.

"I don't know how else to describe it. Whatever it is, it's headed our way. I do not think we are safe here."

Taja left Ravi staring out over the water and went back to the cave to try and coax the others outside. If they weren't safe here then they'd need to move up the beach. But to do that she needed to get the rest of them out of the cave.

She wasn't surprised to see the Wind Elementals of the group already picking their way carefully towards the beach. The wind-gifted were notorious for their claustrophobia. It was more surprising that they'd been able to manage the journey through the tunnels with no problems. Two of the Water Elementals followed tentatively in their wake, while the other water gifted stayed closer to the cave entrance. There was no sign of the Earth or Fire Elementals.

"Don't be afraid," she told the woman and three men just outside the cave. "Can't you smell the water in the air? Why don't you join Ravi down by the water?"

"There's so much of it," the woman whispered.

Taja patted her on the shoulder. "You'll get used to it, I promise."

The three of them looked at her doubtfully, but she gave them what she hoped was a encouraging smile and they finally shuffled off towards the shore. With a sigh she turned and went into the cave. The group huddled together away from the entrance went silent as she entered.

"I know you're afraid," she said, sitting down near them. "And I sympathize, but the purpose for our journey was to escape from the compound. To be free."

"We followed you because we did not wish to die," the spokeswoman for the Earth Elementals told her. "We did not stop to think what would happen at the end of the journey."

"Freedom is not something we ever contemplated before," one of the Fire Elementals said. "We had no need for it. Our lives had purpose. Now we have nothing."

The others murmured in agreement.

"You have your lives," Taja said softly. "And you will find a greater purpose to life than to be used as breeding stock for a madman's experiments. But to do that you must first leave this cave."

"But it is so big and empty out there," a man's voice spoke up. "We will be lost and alone."

"Yes, it is big out there. But it is far from empty, and you are not alone. My people - they're your people too - will do everything they can to help you adjust to your new world. A world where you can make your own decisions, choose your own bed-partners, follow your own path."

There were more murmurings from the group and she waited patiently for them to die down.

"It is, of course, your choice," she said with a shrug, rising to her feet. "You can choose to stay here if you wish, live out your lives in this cave. I can see to it that provisions are dropped off periodically. Or you can come with us and learn what it is to be free. Myself, it has been a long time since I have seen a sunrise, and I don't want to miss this one."

She turned and went back outside, wishing she had more of her sister's sense of diplomacy. Perhaps she'd been a little too blunt, but she didn't know any other way of dealing with them.

The sun was just beginning to crest the horizon as she joined Ravi on the shore. She slipped her hand into his. "Beautiful, isn't it?" she said.

The sky was growing lighter, streaked with pale yellows and oranges that intensified where the sun was rising.

"I have no words," Ravi said. He pulled her closer and kissed her. "Thank you."

"For what?" she asked breathlessly.

"For this," he replied, nodding towards the sunrise. "And for all the sunrises to come."

"Ravi, I--"

There was a shout from the group near the fire. They turned to see what was causing the disturbance and were just able to make out a group making its way slowly along the shoreline towards the fire.

"Is that --"

"Nereida," Ravi whispered.

He seemed frozen in place and Taja had to tug him forward. The sky was just light enough that she could see many of the women in the group were injured, and their leader was carrying someone in his arms. They reached the fire at the same time and Taja could see the man wore a guard's uniform.

"You must be Kairavini - she told us we would find you here," the man said, nodding towards the woman he was holding.

"What have you done to her?" Ravi demanded.

"Here, put her down here," Taja said, spreading out a blanket one of the guards passed her.

The man did so, carefully, and then straightened again.

"He's done nothing but take care of her," one of the women from the group called out. "He's taken care of us all. If it wasn't for him we'd all still be trapped in the compound."

"I would never harm her," he said. "It was her visions. She's been like this since the last one, the one that told her we would find you if we followed the shoreline."

Ravi was already kneeling beside her. He took one slender hand in his. "You must not give up now, my sister. Not when we are finally free of that place."

Nereida stirred and her eyes blinked open. "Kair-avini? Is that truly you?"

"Yes, it truly is." Tears pricked at his eyes.

"The danger is not over," she whispered, eyes closing again. "And we are not the only ones in its path. The water comes."

"What do you mean, the water comes?" Taja asked.

"She's too weak to answer your questions," the guard who was still hovering protectively over Nereida told her. "She needs rest."

"And just who are you to tell us what to do?" Ravi asked angrily.

"His name is Kaine. Without him I would have died long ago." There was a softness to Nereida's voice that had nothing to do with how weak she was.

Kaine sank to his knees in the sand on her other side and, without looking at Ravi, took her free hand in his. "Don't try to talk. You need to rest."

"Ravi," Taja touched his arm. "Even I can see they care for each other. Let me see if I can make contact with my people."

She moved away and bit down with her back molars to activate the E.T.T. "We've reached the other side of the volcano. We need medical assistance and transport."

Negative. Unable to comply.

She couldn't possibly have heard that right, not after all they'd been through to get to this spot. "What do you mean, unable to comply? I have people who need medical assistance!"

Prepare for data transfer.

Data transfer. This was bad. This was very, very bad. A data transfer was only used in times of extreme emergency when a great deal of information needed to be exchanged as quickly as possible.

The data burst hit her like a sledgehammer and she sank to her knees with a cry.

"Taja?" Ravi looked up from where he sat with his sister, ready to come to her aid.

"I'm fine," she said, waving a hand at him to stay. "Just give me a minute."

She took several slow, deep breaths as her mind slowly assimilated the information she received. "Oh, gods and goddesses!"

"What is it?"

Taja looked at Ravi, her face pale in the firelight. "The seismic activity we experienced went deeper than just the volcano. It spread along fault lines under the ocean floor creating fissures and triggering an underwater earthquake."

"But that is not what has you worried," he guessed.

"My people were already monitoring the seismic activity from their ship, otherwise they would not have seen it in time. Unfortunately, they have no Earth Elementals with them - they could have prevented it."

"Taja, tell us what is happening."

By this time the entire group had gathered closer. Taja took a deep breath and stood up again. "The underwater earthquake has caused a massive tsunami, and it's headed our way. Or it will be headed our way shortly. The Water Elementals with my people are working with the Illezie to hold it back to give the transport ships enough time to evacuate the civilian population in its path. The problem is, the longer they hold it back, the more it's building up."

"What about us?" a woman from the back of the group called out.

"They will not be able to free up one of the transport ships in time to come for us. We're on our own."

As the voices erupted around her, Taja sought and held Ravi's gaze. "I'm sorry," she whispered.

Chapter Twenty-Three

From Nereida's Journal:

Kaine grows weaker. He tries to hide it from me but I can tell. Every time he heals me he strengthens the bond between us and weakens himself. I have tried to get him to stop, but he will not listen. It's not that I don't love him, I love him more than I can possibly say. Perhaps even more than I love my brother, although it is, of course, a much different love. But it's just going to make it that much worse for him when I die. If I am fortunate I will see my brother once more and at last feel the sun on my face. I do not fear death, I fear only the pain it will cause those I love. I hope that when they read this they remember that although the body dies, the spirit lives on.

Ravi refused to believe this was the end for them. They had not come this far only to be faced with death now that they were free.

The cave . . .

The whisper filled his mind and he glanced down at his sister. Her eyes were still closed but her hand tightened fractionally in his.

"Nereida?"

U*se the Earth* . . .

"I don't understand."

"What is it?" Taja asked.

He looked up at her. "Nereida is trying to give me a message - something about the cave and using the earth."

"No," Kaine said slowly. "Not the earth, the Earth Elementals. I think she's suggesting we go into a cave and have the Earth Elementals seal us up inside." He looked at them with a kind of grim determination. "She's not always coherent with her visions and I've become adept at deciphering her meaning."

Ravi looked at Taja, who shrugged. "We'd probably have a better chance back in the cave than out here in the open," she said.

"Nereida," he asked, looking down at her again. "Is that what you're saying? We'll be safe if we're sealed up in the cave?"

The others, yes. But not you. You will save us all. You must stop the water.

Ravi looked out over the ocean where the Elementals had the giant wave barely restrained. As much as it pained him to admit it, he had to believe his sister was wrong. What she was asking was impossible.

"What's she telling you?" Taja asked when she could stand it no longer.

Gently releasing his sister's hand, he rose to his feet. "She agrees about the cave."

"And?" she prompted.

He hesitated, then told her the rest. "She seems to believe I have a chance of stopping the water."

"She has faith in your ability, or she's had a vision of you doing it?"

"I don't know. She's very weak and not very co-herent." He glanced down at his sister, clearly worried.

"All right," Taja said briskly. "You two," she indicated two of the guards, "start moving everyone back into the cave. It's the best chance we've got. You," she said to the third guard, "Help Kaine with Nereida."

She made sure everyone started moving and then pulled Ravi aside. "No matter what Nereida said, you don't have to do this."

"Will your people be able to save all those who are in the path of the tsunami?"

Taja looked off towards the sunrise, hesitating.

"Taja." He turned her to face him. "Tell me."

Shoulders slumping, she said, "They have only been able to evacuate about half the population. They started with the people living along the coast first, but the water is projected to travel several miles inland."

Ravi put his arms around her and held her close. She clung to him, resting her head on his shoulder. "I'm staying out here with you."

"No!" He loosened his grip so he could look down at her. "You need to go into the cave with the others so you'll be safe."

Reaching up, she pulled his head down for a long, lingering kiss. "I will not leave you."

"But--"

She place her fingers over his lips to stop him. "I will not leave you," she repeated.

"You are a stubborn woman."

"You have no idea," she said with a grin.

* * * * *

Taja left him watching the sunrise while she went to have a last word with those in the cave. Most of them were settling towards the back of the cavern, probably a wise move.

"I am sorry to have you back in here when you have finally found your way out, but this is the safest place for you to be."

"How long must we wait?" one of the guards asked.

"I don't know. It depends on how fast the tsunami travels once the elementals working with my people release it."

"Then how will we know when it's safe to emerge?" someone else called out.

Taja hadn't considered that. She glanced towards Nereida but Kaine shook his head. It looked like he'd made her as comfortable as possible under the circumstances, but she was still unconscious so she wouldn't be able to talk with Ravi mind to mind. There was no way she could ask one of the Earth Elementals to stay outside with them and they had no working communicators.

"You," she said suddenly to one of the women she recognized as a Water Elemental. "What's your name?"

"Me? I am AE-02--"

"No," Taja said. "Not your designation, your name. None of you ever have to respond to a designation again."

"My name is Avani."

"Okay, Avani. I need you to see if you can connect with the water outside of this cave - just like Kairavini did."

"I can try," Avani said, doubt filling her voice. She closed her eyes and stilled. Keeping her eyes closed, she spoke. "Yes, I can feel the water. It is so vast . . ." All at once her eyes snapped open. "The water, there is something wrong. There is an energy building up in it that should not be there."

"I know," Taja told her. "But this means you should be able to sense when this 'wrongness' is gone, right?"

"I--yes. I should be able to."

"That's good." Taja turned towards the guards that had come with them from the compound. "Once Avani tells you it's safe, have the Earth Elementals unblock the cave entrance again. Whether we succeed or fail, a transport ship will be coming to pick everyone up."

She went back to the mouth of the cave and the Earth Elementals grouped there. "You know what to do?"

The spokeswoman nodded. "We will use our combined strength to seal the opening tightly so that nothing can get through."

"Great. Do it as soon as I'm clear of the entrance."

"We will. Good luck to you both."

"Thank you," Taja said. She had a feeling they were going to need all the luck they could get.

* * * * *

Kairavini could sense the build up of water, almost half a world away. And he could sense the other Water Elementals as they strained to control it. Two of them had already fallen, their inner resources depleted. Why did they not try to subdue it, rather than contain it?

"No," he whispered. "This is wrong."

Whatever they were doing, they were only making matters worse. There was a storm out over the ocean - an unnatural storm fueled by elemental energies. There was wind, of course, but somehow there was fire as well, only twisted in some way that he was unable to figure out. It was affecting the tsunami, changing it.

Ravi felt Taja return to his side, but he was unable to tear his eyes away from the light of the rising sun, shimmering on the water. She slipped her hand into his and he laced his fingers between hers.

A plethora of conflicting emotions churned inside him. He burned with the need to be with this woman while at the same time fearing for her safety. This was something he should be facing alone, but he was glad she was with him. He wished Nereida was awake and able to tell him what was the matter with him.

This is what it means to love, a female voice whispered through his mind.

Nereida?

There was no answer. Perhaps he'd only imagined her voice in his head.

"I would be happier if you were in the cave with the others," he said at last, looking down at Taja. "If I am unable to halt the water . . ."

She was already shaking her head. "Whatever happens, we will face it together."

A noise from behind had them turning in tandem to see the earth around the mouth of the cave shiver and then draw inward until the cavern was sealed tightly.

"There," she said with a hint of satisfaction. "No getting rid of me now."

Unable to help himself, he pulled her into his arms. "I could not bear it if anything happened to you."

"Nothing will happen to me," she murmured against his chest.

"I wish I was as sure. To find you, only to lose you now . . ."

Raising her head, she gripped him by the shoulders and gave him a little shake. "You are not going to lose me! I have not waited a life time to find you, only to give up because of a little water."

He looked at her in disbelief. "A little water? We--"

She stopped him by pulling his head down for a passionate kiss. Ravi groaned under the soft, but insistent onslaught, caught up for just a moment before reality intruded and he pulled away.

"What are you doing?"

"Kissing you," she said. "We don't have time for anything more. My contact on the ship said the Water Elementals have lost control of the tsunami."

Ravi's heart ached with love for this woman. It had to be love. From what he'd read there was no other emotion that could tie a person in so many knots.

Tell her you idiot!

"I love you," he said simply, not even questioning the voice in his head. "With you at my side there is nothing I cannot face - Dr. Arjun, the volcano, or even a wall of water. And if we are not meant to survive what is coming, then my soul will follow yours to the afterlife."

There were tears in her eyes as she cupped his cheek with her palm. "I love you, Kairavini. You are mine and I am yours, now and forever."

He kissed her again, trying to impart every ounce of emotion that had been bottled up inside him for so many years. Then gently he moved her to one side. "I know better than to ask you to stand behind me, so I ask instead that you stand beside me."

"Always," she said.

Focusing on the water in front of him, he submersed his consciousness into the ocean, joining with it. His awareness broadened. With a single thought he was able to read the currents, the pull of the tides - the onrushing tsunami that was greater than it had any right to be. He could feel the unnatural energies suffusing it and knew he would not be able to control it through will alone.

All this he learned in a single heartbeat. In the next he began formulating his plan. First he stilled the waves in front of them, bending them to his will. Up and down the coast the water stilled, while further out waves began to build, racing outwards, building in volume.

Seeking further he met the unnatural energy of the tsunami. It twisted and pulled, distorting the water on a molecular level. He sent healing energy streaking towards it, stabilizing the water molecules, driving out the unwanted energies so that they hissed and boiled in a cloud of steam.

The tsunami raced forward, diminished with the loss of negative energy, but no less dangerous. Ravi began building on his own wave, sending it hurtling to meet it. The two waves met with a resounding crack that they felt right down to their bones. Ravi frantically began pulling energy from the returning backwash. Though most of the farmlands had been saved, their own lives were still in question.

He pulled Taja tightly to his side and with the remainder of his strength gathered the water molecules in the air closer around them and hardened them.

The water struck.

Chapter Twenty-Four

From Nereida's Journal:

Sta'at says it will not be much longer. She has taken over my body so that I can make this one, final, entry. So many things I wish to say, but there is not enough time. My dearly loved brother, Kairavini. My greatest wish is that you do not let yourself be overcome by despair at my passing. You have so much to live for! Embrace the love you have been given and never let go. I see much happiness for you and Taja, the children you will have together. And if you have not already found her by the time you read this, seek out our younger sister Rayne. Mother died so that Rayne should not suffer the life we had, and she has become a woman worthy of that sacrifice. And finally, my brother, be kind to my beloved Kaine. His love sustained me through my pain and suffering, he was the light to my darkest days.

Ravi could feel every rock and stone and piece of driftwood underneath him. It was not a pleasant feeling but he couldn't seem to muster the energy to move. After another minute or so he cracked his eyes open, squinting into the sun shining down on him. Something moved to block the sun from his face.

"Ravi? Are you all right?"

"Taja?" he guessed, still not able to see properly. "Did it work?"

"Of course it worked," she said, half laughing and half crying. "Did you have any doubts that it wouldn't?"

He could feel drops on his face. "Then why the tears, beloved?"

"Oh, Ravi!"

His question seemed to make her cry harder so he pulled her down on top of him for a kiss. It was a very long, very satisfying kiss and just as he almost managed to muster enough energy to roll her over underneath him, she pulled away.

"I thought I'd lost you, that you'd burned yourself out saving us."

"The water is at peace now, though I think it will be some time before I am able to create another wave of that size."

Taja helped him to sit up and he stared around in amazement. Already the sun was drying the sand. "How long was I unconscious?"

"A couple of hours." She grinned suddenly. "Whatever you did to protect us worked. We're the only things on the beach that didn't get a good wetting."

He cupped her face with the palm of his hand and then leaned over to kiss her. "We did it," he whispered against her lips.

"You mean you did it."

"I think we should celebrate," he said between kisses that were getting increasingly more insistent.

"What did you have in mind," she asked, breath quickening.

His hands went to the fastenings of her shirt. "Why don't I show you?"

There was a rumbling behind them and they turned to see the entrance to the cave opening up again. Ravi heaved a sigh. "I could wish they had better timing."

Taja laughed. "We have the rest of our lives to celebrate."

"The rest of our lives . . ." His fingers traced across her cheek and over her lips. "I like the sound of that."

She kissed his fingers and then got to her feet, pulling him up beside her.

Two of the guards led the group back out of the cave. The M-class who'd accompanied Nereida were the bravest, passing the guards and spreading out in twos and threes along the beach. They were followed by the Water Elementals who seemed rather fearful as they glanced from the water to Ravi and back again.

"What is the matter with you?" he asked, unnerved by the way they were watching him.

"We could feel it," Avani whispered. "We could sense the water. Feel your power as you bent it to your will."

The awe in her voice made him distinctly uncomfortable.

"Are we safe now?" one of the guards asked.

Ravi turned to Taja, who'd contacted her people again.

"Yes," she assured them. "There is a transport on its way. They'll take us to the ship that's in orbit and our injuries will be taken care of."

"What of Dr. Arjun?" one of the M class called out. "Has he been found?"

"No, but we believe we know where his new compound is and it's only a matter of time."

Bringing up the rear of the group was Kaine, cradling Nereida in his arms as though she was made of glass. She was wrapped in a blanket and he made his way carefully to a spot where there was a rise of the sand to support her back so that she could see out over the water.

He laid her down gently and looked up apologetically at Ravi. "I would not have moved her, but she insisted she wanted to be outside of the cave."

"Nereida," Ravi scolded, kneeling beside her on the sand. "You should not have asked Kaine to bring you out here, you need to focus your energy on feeling well again."

"I wanted to feel the sun on my face, at least once," Nereida whispered.

Kaine tried to move away to give them some privacy but her hand tightened on his. "I need you both at my side."

"Save your strength, my sister. Taja says there is a shuttle on the way to take us to a ship where you can be seen to."

"My strength is only borrowed - Kaine knows."

Ravi looked over at Kaine. "What is she talking about?"

"My race are known as empaths," Kaine said quietly. "But what is not known is that in a very few individuals that empathy can translate into a healing energy. I have been sharing this energy with Nereida."

"Healing? But why?" He looked down at his sister but her eyes were closed, an ethereal smile on her face.

"From the first time I saw Nereida, I knew she was dying."

"Dying! But how -- the visions," Ravi said, feeling sick inside.

"Yes." Kaine nodded. "Each time she had a vision she grew weaker, took longer to recover."

"But there must be something we can do. If we get her to the ship--"

I*t is not to be, my brother.*

Ravi felt a chill of fear race up his spine. *Don't talk like that!*

B*e kind to Kaine. He is alone and will need a friend.*
N*ereida, no!*

There was a burst of energy in his mind, the sensation of her all around him, and then she was gone.

"Nereida!"

"No!" Kaine's howl of anguish echoed Ravi's.

Taja's heart ached for the two men bent over the frail form lying so still on the sand. There was nothing she could do for either of them. She'd never felt so helpless. The others began drawing closer.

"Please," she said. "Give them some room."

There was sniffling and quiet tears from the rest of the M-class. Nereida had been their friend and leader and inspiration. Without her some of them would not have been able to endure.

The rest of the group stayed back out of respect.

"She--she fought to stay with us, to feel the sun on her face at last," Kaine said brokenly to Ravi. "She needed to see you one last time to say goodbye." He broke down completely at this, unashamed of the tears on his face.

Taja knelt on the sand at Nereida's head. "She loved you both," she said quietly.

Ravi looked at her, unable to speak. There was a hollowness to his eyes that sent a shiver through her. It was like he had lost his soul.

"Forgive me," one of the former security guards said quietly. "But we have company."

Taja felt a flash of anger. Of course the rescue would come too late. After all Ravi had done to save this world - he deserved better than to have his sister die right in front of him.

She looked up - and froze.

* * * *

Ravi was only dimly aware of what was being said around him. He felt cold and numb inside, like he'd never feel warm again. There was a hole inside him where Nereida should be. It was like he'd been ripped in two.

He felt Taja's hand on his shoulder, heard her speaking his name to draw him back from the abyss in his mind. Something in her tone finally registered.

Raising his head he felt the frisson of fear running through the group surrounding them. Automatically he reached out to the water, but it was still at peace. Something else then. Then he became conscious of what the others were muttering.

Allowing Taja to help to his feet he stared at the small group making their way down the beach towards them.

"Arjun!" He spat the name like the curse it was.

Kaine got slowly to his feet, moving over to stand at his left side. Taja stood on his right, her hold going from his hand to his arm. Her grip was tight but he hardly felt it.

"Everyone stay where you are," one of the dozen guards with Arjun called out.

The advancing guards were heavily armed and their weapons were drawn. They stopped several yards away.

"You're fortunate we found you," Arjun said. "We've had casualties in our move to the new location and there are gaps to be filled. Cullen, check designations."

The head of Arjun's security detached himself from the rest and with a swagger approached the group. Several of his men trailed after him; most of the M-class backed away. Ravi could feel the tension coming off Kaine and glanced at him, shocked at the look of intense hatred on the man's face as he watched the security chief.

"What is it?" he whispered. "Is it something to do with Nereida?"

Kaine gave a short nod. "He enjoys tormenting women - especially the weak and helpless."

Anger began coiling inside Ravi.

"These ones over here appear to be M-class," Cullen called to Dr. Arjun.

"Time to separate the wheat from the chaff," Arjun replied. "All of you mistakes, over there." He gestured with his weapon towards the mountain side of the shore. Without hesitation the group that had accompanied Nereida shuffled off to the side.

Cullen began calling out the designations for the rest of the group and Arjun made the decision whether they were to join the M-class or move to the other side of the beach. Ravi could feel the tension rising in Taja's touch as the guards worked their way towards them. Finally, only Ravi was left and when Cullen approached Kaine stepped into his path.

"Out of my way," Cullen ordered.

"So brave, holding a weapon on an unarmed man," Kaine taunted. "Just like you were so manly abusing the women you've been with."

"I don't need a laser to deal with you," Cullen sneered. With his free hand he pulled out a knife and thrust it upwards into Kaine's torso. Kaine's mouth opened but no sound came out as he sank to the sand.

"Kaine!"

The water in the bay was no longer at peace.

Ravi heard Taja's gasp of shock as Kaine fell. Then she was pushed aside as two of Cullen's men came up behind him, holding him in place. Cullen grabbed his wrist and read the designation on it, a triumphant smile on his face.

"This is the one you were looking for," he called to Dr. Arjun.

"You . . ." Arjun's voice was dry and cracked. "AE-03-85-07. You are my greatest triumph. You are my proof that I am right. You are the first stage in the creation of the perfect Elemental."

"You're wrong," Ravi said, pulling away from the men holding him. "My name is Kairavini, and I am my own man!"

Waves began crashing onto the shore.

"Bring them," Arjun ordered, nodding towards the small cluster of men and women Cullen had separated out from the group. "Kill the rest."

"No!" Taja yelled. "You can't do this!"

"Including the traitorous guards." Arjun lifted the laser pistol he was carrying and fired.

"Taja! No!"

The water in the bay shot upwards in a multitude of geysers as Ravi ripped free of the guards and fell to the sand beside Taja. Dr. Arjun's face wore an intense expression of satisfaction.

"What power you possess! From you will spring a line of Elementals like no other."

Ravi ignored him. "Taja, I cannot lose you too," he said, lowering his voice for only her to hear. He reached out, not sure whether he should touch her or not. There was so much blood he wasn't even sure where exactly she'd been hit. Tenderly he brushed a strand of hair from her face.

"You see now why I wished to train emotions out of you?" Arjun demanded. "They only cause pain and confusion. I will find a way to breed emotion right out of future generations."

"You have to stop him," Taja whispered.

"How? I have no weapon."

"You are an Elemental, you are never without a weapon," she said, eyes closing. "Remember your training."

"Guards!" Dr. Arjun demanded. "You have your orders. Dispose of those we're leaving behind and bring the others."

"No!" Ravi said, climbing to his feet. The water in the bay stilled again, as quickly as it had erupted. Even the waves that had been lapping against the shore stilled under his subconscious command.

Whatever the guards saw in his face had them backing away from him. Ravi recalled the lessons in his element, how they learned to pull water from the very air around them. And he recalled his lessons in bio-chemistry, of the percentage of the body that was water.

"I will not allow this. *We* will not allow this." He gestured towards the other Elementals and they moved towards each other, forming a group again.

"Call off your guards," he ordered, voice deadly calm.

"Don't be ridiculous. You will either come peacefully or be dragged along, it makes no difference either way, but you will be coming with me."

"I don't think so," Ravi said quietly.

He gathered his focus, staring intently at the man before him. With his mind he could feel the water molecules in the breeze coming off the ocean, but he pushed them aside. He narrowed his target, seeking the water binding the chemicals in the body standing so arrogantly on the shore.

"You!" Arjun gasped. "What are you doing?"

"Is that fear I see in your eyes?" Ravi asked, with some small sense of satisfaction.

"I demand you stop whatever it is you're doing!"

"In case you haven't noticed, you and your men are in no position to demand anything. Call off your men and leave us in peace."

"Never!

"Then you leave me no choice."

Cullen made a move towards Ravi but was driven off as a wind sprang up, blowing swirls of sand and debris at him. As he backed further away several of the M-class tentatively moved forward, then rushed him all at once using driftwood and rocks and their bare hands to attack him.

Ravi ignored the disturbance as the Elementals used their gifts and the M-class used whatever came to hand to fight the guards. His attention was centered on Dr. Arjun. His concentration focused on the molecules of water he was slowly drawing towards him.

"No! Stop!" Arjun gasped, his lips parched and cracking. He swayed in place, seeming somehow diminished. "Please . . ."

Unmoved, Ravi continued to pull the moisture from Arjun's body. The doctor's form shrank further, collapsing in on itself. He was no longer able to talk, no longer able to make any sound at all other than a long, drawn out wailing sigh as what was left of him crumpled to the ground.

Kairavini stared at the dried out husk of what used to be the most powerful man in his universe, and felt nothing. No hatred, no satisfaction - they would not erase the pain this man had caused, nor would they bring back those he had killed.

"Look!" someone from behind called out.

Ravi raised his head to see a large ship settling on the beach a few hundred yards away. What did it matter now? He'd already lost everything. It was quiet on the beach and he looked around, surprised to see that the guards had been subdued. Several were struggling in holes that had been opened up under them by the Earth Elementals and then closed up again. Several more were dead at the hands of the M-class and the rest had been herded into a small group off to the side.

Kneeling down beside Taja again, he was stunned to see she was still breathing. Kaine had somehow managed to drag himself up beside her, his hand resting on her wound.

"I have her stabilized for now," Kaine gasped. "But my energy is so low it will not last for long."

Tears of gratitude filled Ravi's eyes. "But how--"

"Could not save Nereida . . . save who I can . . . too much loss today . . ."

Kaine's eyes closed as those closest around them shouted for the approaching group to hurry.

Chapter Twenty-Five

In those first few days after, Ravi refused to leave Taja's side, as though afraid that if he let her out of his sight he'd lose her too. Fortunately she didn't have to stay long in the med-wing and her sister Nakeisha arranged for quarters for them aboard the Valkyrie starship.

The rest of Dr. Arjun's men had been rounded up and those they were guarding were released. As the ambassador for Ardraci, Nakeisha had her hands full dealing with the Breeders, Seeders, and children that survived the program. There was technically nothing they could do with the guards Arjun had hired, but she let the authorities deal with the medical staff.

There was a soft knock on the door to the quarters they'd been assigned and Taja shot a quick glance towards Ravi before getting up answer it. He sat unmoving in a chair facing the view port, staring blankly at the stars streaming by, as he had every day since she recovered enough to be released from the med-wing.

He'd been sinking further and further into depression and she was at a loss how to help him. It had become worse since they'd received the news that when the burial detail had returned to the beach to take care of the bodies there, there had been no trace of Nereida. It was believed she had more of the water gift than anyone realized and she'd returned to her element.

"How is he?" Nakeisha whispered, when Taja opened the door.

Taja shook her head. "You can speak mind to mind with Chaney, correct?"

"It is not easy for us, but yes."

"Imagine how you would feel if you could speak to him all your life and he was suddenly ripped away. Imagine feeling him die."

Nakeisha shuddered. "It does not bear thinking of."

"Let's talk outside," Taja suggested, shooting another glance at Ravi, although he didn't appear to be aware of them.

"I'm afraid I'm losing him," she blurted, once the door slid shut behind him.

"Taja, no. He just needs time--" She reached a hand out to her sister.

"He's getting worse with time, not better." Taja shrugged off Nakeisha's comforting hand and paced away a few steps.

"Everyone mourns differently . . ."

"That's just it. He hasn't mourned."

"What?"

Taja whirled back to face her. "He hasn't shed one tear for her. He won't talk about her - he just stares at me if I try to bring her name up. He won't even talk to the few survivors from his year group I've managed to track down. Have you had any luck?"

Nakeisha shook her head. "I'm sorry. It does not appear as though any of his offspring survived."

As near as they'd been able to figure out, there had been more than two thousand people on board the ship that had fled from Ardraci. Now the colony was down to just a few hundred and of that only five were with Arjun from the beginning.

"What am I going to do?"

"I do not mean to interrupt but I would very much like to speak with Kairavini."

Taja whirled around with a gasp. "Kaine! You scared the life out of me!"

"Forgive me, that was not my intention."

She smiled weakly. "It's all right. A shot of adrenalin every once in awhile does the body good. And speaking of good, you're looking fit. How are you feeling?"

He bowed slightly. "I am well, thank you."

He was very pale, but she wondered if that was his natural coloring. His face bore lines it hadn't before and his eyes were haunted. He, too, was in mourning. But at least he was dealing with it.

"You can go on in, but don't be surprised if you don't get a response. He's . . . having a bit of trouble dealing with all this."

* * * * *

Kaine smiled his thanks as Taja opened the door for him. It slid closed gently behind him and he turned to the man slumped in the chair. Head cocked, he studied him for a moment before speaking.

"You realize you dishonor her by shutting down like this."

Ravi gave a start, as though he hadn't realized he wasn't alone. His eyes narrowed when he saw who was standing there. "What would you know about honor? You just used her like everyone else."

"I'm sorry you think so," Kaine said quietly, refused to rise to the bait.

"No, I'm the one who's sorry. You saved Taja, almost dying yourself in the process. For that I will always be grateful." He gestured towards a second chair that was set up facing the view port. "Please."

Kaine hesitated, then shook his head. "Another time perhaps. Today I am here to fulfill a promise I made." He pulled a slim, leather bound book from his breast pocket. "This was Nereida's journal. She wanted you to have it."

Ravi reached out slowly, tentatively, and took it from him. "I didn't even know she kept a journal."

"She started it just a few weeks before we began our journey through the volcano. More of a memoire than a journal, I believe."

Ravi glanced up at him sharply. "You believe? You mean you haven't read it?"

Kaine shook his head. "I did not need to. She told me most of what's in it, and the rest was for you. Towards the end, when holding a pen became too much effort, she had me write the entries for her." He faltered. "It was not an easy thing to do."

* * * * *

Taja came back into the room as Kaine left, curious as to what he'd had to say to Ravi.

"Kaine looks good, considering the damage Cullen's knife did to him, don't you think?" she asked. "And it's wonderful that all of the M-class are so willing to keep the secret of his healing abilities."

Ravi still sat in his chair, focused on the slim leather-bound book that he kept turning around and around in his hands. He looked up at her, eyes glistening.

"Kaine gave this to me. It was Nereida's."

Taja went over and knelt at his side.

"What is it?" she asked softly.

"He said . . . he said it was her journal. Her life's story." A tear tracked its way down his face. "It's so thin . . . just like she was. A person's life shouldn't have so few pages."

His breath caught as he choked back a sob. Taja gently took the book from him and set it aside, then moved up into his lap. "Let it out," she whispered, pulling him into her arms.

Though her heart broke anew for Ravi, Taja couldn't help feeling relief as the wall he'd built around his emotions came crumbling down.

When his grief finally abated and he loosened his hold, Taja shifted in his lap and wiped the tears from both their faces.

"I am sorry I never had the chance to meet her properly," she said softly.

Ravi gave her a ghost of a smile. "I think you would have become great friends. She already liked you from what she saw through my eyes."

"It must have been hard for you both, growing up and not being allowed to acknowledge each other."

"It was, at times. But being able to speak mind to mind made up for it." His voice trailed off as he realized he would never speak mind to mind again.

They were silent for a time, watching the stars streaming by, then Ravi stirred again. "Nereida is the one who insisted I help you. She believed you had a great purpose for being in the compound, and she was right." He tightened his hold on her. "She knew we were meant to be together."

"Nereida was a very wise woman," Taja said with a smile.

There was a knock on the door. Taja looked at Ravi. "It's probably my sister again. Are you feeling up to company?"

"I think . . . yes, I think company would be good. Your sister has a soothing presence."

Taja gave him a kiss before sliding off his lap and going to the door. It was indeed Nakeisha on the other side, along with a young woman who looked strangely familiar.

"I'm sorry to bring someone without asking first, but I thought you'd forgive me, under the circumstances," Nakeisha said.

"What circumstances?" Taja asked. She frowned at the young woman hesitating on the threshold. "Don't I know you from somewhere?"

"Taja, this is --"

"Rayne!" Ravi exclaimed. He'd risen to his feet and was facing the door. "I'm happy to see you escaped the compound before the volcano destroyed it."

"It is nice to see you as well, Kairavini." Rayne smiled tentatively at him.

"What is it?" he asked Taja. She had a peculiar look on her face and was looking back and forth between him and Rayne.

"Is she . . . ?"

Nakeisha nodded. "Ravi, I . . ." she looked helplessly at her sister.

"Ravi, I had Nakeisha do a check to see if you had any living offspring from the program. Unfortunately, none survived."

"While it is disappointing, it is not surprising. Remember, I saw all those files with the red stamps. I guessed their meaning."

"But although we didn't find any children," Nakeisha said, "I did find a younger sibling."

"Sibling? But that--" He was about to say that was impossible, that their mother had died, but then he took a closer look at Rayne. Once again he was struck by her resemblance to Nereida. A healthier, happier Nereida. When he first met her he put it down to her being a Water Elemental, but now . . .

"Nereida, she knew. I think she may have even tried to tell me once."

"I know I can never replace the sister you lost . . ."

He took a step closer, eyes searching her face. "You look very much like she did," he whispered. "I don't know why I didn't see it before."

They stood staring at each other, not even aware that Taja and Nakeisha had left the room.

"She had visions," Ravi said. "I think she had visions of you, but there was never enough time to talk about them."

"I hope some day you'll be able to tell me about her."

He glanced down at the journal he'd picked up without thinking about it. He was only beginning to realize how little how little he knew of his twin. "Why don't we learn about our sister . . . together?"

About the Author

Residing in Cobourg, Ontario, Carol has always had a love of reading and writing. She grew up reading Edgar Rice Burroughs and Robert E. Howard so it's no wonder her first love is fantasy, followed closely by science fiction.

She always believed she was meant to be a writer of short stories, however her stories tended to be rather long. They also tended to have a romantic thread running through them. Finally caving in to the inevitable, she embraced her genre and began writing novels of fantasy/science fiction adventure with a dash of romance thrown into the mix. She has never regretted it.

Today she writes a variety of prose: non-fiction, flash fiction, short stories, and novels – in a variety of genres: humour, horror, contemporary, romance, science fiction, and fantasy. She's also a prolific poet.

Visit Carol on her blog at: http://www.random-writerlythoughts.blogpot.com She can also be found as Carol R. Ward on Facebook and CarolRWard on Twitter.

Other Books by the Author

An Elemental Wind
(Ardraci Elementals)

An Elemental Fire
(Ardraci Elementals)

Magical Misfire
(The Moonstone Chronicles)

Made in the USA
Charleston, SC
05 June 2014